Reviewers said this about
Lilith:
Demon of the Night

A Detective Louis Martelli, NYPD, Mystery

"Fast paced with snappy dialogue, likeable characters, and a touch of Middle Eastern mythology, this is a book that I could really sink my teeth into."
Paige Lovitt for *Reader Views*

"With more twists and turns than a Boa constrictor, the venomous plot unfolds and transports the reader from a modern-day, high-tech crime fighting novel into the dark side of cult practices within the mind of a serial murderer fixated on revenge. *Lilith* is a trophy on any shelf."
Gary Sorkin for *Pacific Book Review*

"Given the real-life vampire cases cited in the novel, one has to wonder if this isn't another of Cohen's 'ripped-from-the-headline' stories. Why aren't Hollywood producers calling about this gem?"
Irene Watson, Author of *The Sitting Swing* and *Rewriting Life Scripts*

"I've had a fascination with vampires ever since Italian researchers believe they found the remains of a female vampire from 16th-century Venice, buried with a brick in her mouth to prevent her feasting on plague victims. This macabre thriller will keep you on the edge of your chair to the very end."
Susan Violante, Author of *Innocent War: Behind An Immigrant's Past*
italianaustinite.com, blogtalkradio.com/vioradio

For more information, visit:
www.theodore-cohen-novels.com

Other Novels
by
Theodore Jerome Cohen

*Death by Wall Street**
*House of Cards**
Frozen in Time†
Unfinished Business†
End Game†
Cold Blood††
Full Circle

* A Detective Louis Martelli, NYPD, Mystery/Thriller
†The Antarctic Murders Trilogy
††The Antarctic Murders Trilogy, Books I, II, III in one Kindle eBook edition

Visit us on the World Wide Web
http://www.theodore-cohen-novels.com

Lilith

Demon of the Night

Theodore Jerome Cohen

TJC Press

TJC Press
122 Shady Brook Drive
Langhorne, PA 19047-8027 USA
www.theodore-cohen-novels.com

First published 1/13/2012

Library of Congress Control Number: 2011944845

ISBN-10: 0984920994 (sc)
ISBN-13: 978-0-9849209-9-0 (sc)
ISBN-10: 0-9849209-0-0 (e)
ISBN-13: 978-0-9849209-0-7 (e)

Published in the United States of America

Front cover design by eBookConversion.com

Photo Credits:
Cover and interior photographs: Big Stock Photo
Photograph of author: Susan Cohen, 2007

The views expressed in this work are solely those of the author.

Printed by CreateSpace, An Amazon.com Company
Available from Amazon.com, CreateSpace.com, and other retail outlets

Available on Kindle
eBook created by eBookConversion.com

Copyrights
and
Other Notes and Notices

Abbreviations

1PP	One Police Plaza (Police Department Headquarters, New York City)
24x7	Twenty-Four by Seven (Around the Clock, Seven Days a Week)
ADA	Assistant District Attorney
AM	Ante Meridiem; Before Midday
CBC	Complete Blood Count
CDO	Collateralized Debt Obligation
CSI	Crime Scene Investigator
CSU	Crime Scene Unit
DA	District Attorney
DC	District of Columbia
DMV	Department of Motor Vehicles
DNA	Deoxyribonucleic Acid
DWS	Driving While Short
FBI	Federal Bureau of Investigation
FDA	Food and Drug Administration
HIPAA	Health Insurance Portability and Accountability Act (Privacy Rule)
ID	Identification
IT	Information Technology
MO	Missouri
MP	Military Police
NJ	New Jersey
NY	New York
NYPD	New York Police Department
PC	Personal Computer
PC	Politically Correct
PM	Post Meridiem; After Midday
R&R	Rest and Relaxation
SEC	Securities and Exchange Commission
SOP	Standard Operating Procedure
SUV	Sport Utility Vehicle
US	United States
UV	Ultraviolet
VA	US Department of Veterans Affairs
WI	Wisconsin

Acronyms

ASAP   As Soon As Possible
BOLO   Be On the Lookout (for)

Codes

10-4   Police Ten Code ('acknowledgement')
10-10   Possible Crime
10-64   Quality of Life Incident (Q: Foul Odor)

To those who, like literary historian Susan Sellers, place the current vampire myth in the 'comparative safety of nightmare fantasy.'

■

"There are such beings as vampires, some of us have evidence that they exist. Even had we not the proof of our own unhappy experience, the teachings and the records of the past give proof enough for sane peoples."

Abraham 'Bram' Stoker
Author
Dracula (1897)

■

Acknowledgements

Susan, my wife, provided vital suggestions, insightful editing, and most importantly, unswerving support during the development of the manuscript. She is, and always will be, the love of my life, my soulmate, and my 'partner in crime.' Bob Mehta of eBookConversion.com provided many useful suggestions regarding the production of the Kindle and EBUP versions as well as other guidance pertaining to the distribution of the book. The editorial assistance of Officer Sy Nankin, Essex County (NJ) Sheriff's Department, is gratefully acknowledged.

One

ew York Police Detective Louis Martelli pulled his unmarked *Crown Vic* to the curb in front of the Church of the Holy Redeemer in Lower Manhattan, blocking the funeral procession's lead vehicle and further heightening the tension among the people on the sidewalk. The funeral director, family, and mourners, puzzled by the unusual turn of events, stood there, conversing quietly. Occasionally, someone glanced nervously at the church's entrance. None, however, was allowed back into the building. Two police officers moved among them, rapidly gathering names and other information in preparation for handing their notes to the lead detective—Martelli—for follow-up.

Martelli lifted his left leg over the driver-side door threshold, something necessitated by an old Iraqi War injury. Once out of his car, he made his way up the steps and into the sanctuary. Walking hurriedly toward the altar, he stopped briefly at a point halfway down the aisle, steadied himself on a pew, genuflected, and made the Sign of the Cross before proceeding to the casket.

"Well, well, well, if it ain't Mrs. Martelli's *wunderkind,* Master Sergeant Louis Martelli . . . war hero, Master Detective, and all-about-town *bon vivant!* The last time I saw you and Antonetti together you were chasing the Headless Horseman in Central Park. Remember? It was the

1

case of the serial killer who sliced and diced that pharmaceutical executive behind the Delacourt Theater."

Crime scene investigator Robin Peterson loved to spar with Martelli. A flirt who wore her flaming red hair long, stringy, and parted in the middle, she never let an opportunity go by to tease him.

"People at headquarters are still wondering about you two," she chortled, referring to Martelli and Deputy Coroner Michael Antonetti, who was examining the embalmed remains of an elderly man lying in a coffin to the front of the altar. "Are you two a couple, or aren't you? That's the $64,000 question."

Martelli laughed. "Peterson, are you still knifing guys in the back on Saturday nights so you'll get called to crime scenes and have something to do other than sit at home watching old movies? I mean, when was the last time you had a date?"

Antonetti scowled. "Come on, you two, have a little respect for the dead. This is a holy place of worship!" He was in the last stages of examining the remains in a coffin that was mounted on a mobile display cart.

Peterson resumed her work, taking pictures of the area around the casket and looking for evidence on the floor around it.

Martelli approached Antonetti. "Pardon me for asking, Michael, but what are we doing here? Obviously, the deceased is dead, he's been embalmed, and this *was* a funeral service intended to send him on his way to the Great Beyond. Yet, here we are, some of New York's Finest . . . one of New York City's most skilled deputy coroners, *the* best CSI in the business—he winked at Peterson—and Manhattan's top Detective-Investigator. You would think someone's been shot!"

"He was."

"Who?"

"The deceased."

"You gotta to be kidding! When?"

"Based on what I was told, some time in the last hour or so."

"Come on, Antonetti. The guy's been dead for days."

"I didn't say he was alive when he was shot."

"This isn't another one of your pranks, is it?"

"Nope. I may have pulled a few mischievous tricks in my day—"

"'Mischievous tricks?' Is that what you call them? Like the time you put a fake severed hand covered with blood in my car's trunk—"

Antonetti waved him off. "A childish prank to be sure, Louis. But this is the real thing. The man's been shot . . . the bullet was fired at close range, right through the casket, by someone who apparently came to pay their respects."

"Well, they sure had a strange way of doing it.

"Who discovered the bullet hole?"

"The funeral director, just as he was closing the casket in preparation for moving it to the hearse. That's when he asked everyone to step outside and wait while he called the police."

"And nobody heard anything?"

Peterson looked up. "Before you ask, Martelli, I already grabbed, bagged, and marked as evidence the video tapes from the church's surveillance system. Maybe Dugan'll be able to figure out what happened."

"Thanks, Red.

"Anything else you can tell me, Michael?"

3

"I may be able to say more once I get the corpse back to the morgue. But there is one more thing you should know. It has to do with something I never expected to find."

"What's that?"

"Someone, probably the shooter, stuffed a piece of garlic into the corpse's mouth."

"Garlic?"

"Yes. It's an old Romanian ritual used to ensure a vampire doesn't rise from the dead."

"Oh, that's just great! The next thing you're gonna tell me is that the slug is made of silver!"

"Those generally are used to kill werewolves, Louis, but I guess they'd work on vampires as well."

<u>**Two**</u>

'W'addaya got for me, Missy?" Missy Dugan was a senior information technology specialist in Police Plaza One, or 1PP as the *cognoscenti* called it. She was busy reviewing the videotapes that had been recorded in the sanctuary of the Church of the Holy Redeemer on the afternoon of the funeral service.

It now was 7 in the morning on the day after the funeral had been scheduled to take place. Martelli had just come from his morning workout in Brooklyn's Dominant Fitness & Health Club. Weightlifting mixed with a strenuous aerobics program was the only way he could keep his 6-foot, 2-inch, 190-pound body from succumbing to the unhealthy food he often was forced to eat on the job.

"Antonetti sent the slug to Ballistics. I have the results. As you might expect, it's copper-clad, not silver. I hope the garlic works, or we're in a heap of trouble!" She laughed.

"I wish Antonetti would keep his big mouth shut!"

"Well, it's not every day that someone puts a slug into a vampire, Lou."

Martelli scowled. "I could have told you it wasn't silver. It's too soft for use in ammunition. Unless you had a hard cast with low silver content, firing a silver bullet could really damage your firearm.

"So, were you able to match the slug to anything in the FBI's ballistics' database?"

"Yes. But it's not going to help you."

"I can't tell you how thrilled that makes me!" The exasperated look on his face was obvious.

"Well, I can tell you this . . . it was fired from a 9mm handgun. And—" She paused for impact. "The weapon was used to commit another murder a year ago, a murder that still hasn't been solved."

Martelli's eyes opened wide.

"Which case is that?"

"It's the Hayes shooting. Here, I pulled the file for you."

She took a folder from her workbench and handed it to him.

While Martelli leafed through the folder, Dugan filled him in. "The guy was found on the Upper West Side, face-down in Riverside Park near 103rd Street. You may not remember it because it was handled by the guys in the 24th Precinct. It didn't make much of a splash in the papers at the time because of some sex scandal involving a presidential candidate."

"They call that news?"

Martelli leafed through the file.

"Hmmm...one shot through the heart, close range. Looks pretty straightforward. The responding officer wrote it up as a robbery gone bad."

He set the file down and turned back to her. "I know it's early, but have you had a chance to review the videotapes from the church?"

"Of course, my liege. Some of us work while guys like you lounge around in a gym half the day, flexing your muscles and ogling the chicks!"

"Hey! I didn't have to come to work for this. If I wanted abuse, I would have stayed home!"

"Watch this." Missy swung her chair around and tapped several commands into her computer's keyboard. Instantly, one of several monitors lit up with the video taken by a camera that looked down on the altar from a vantage point near the ceiling of the sanctuary.

"The time is around 12:13 PM. What you're looking at is a shot of the funeral director and one of his men wheeling the casket in for the service, which probably was supposed to start around 1 PM."

"Okay, I see that."

"There . . . the casket's in position." Missy pointed at the monitor. "And here comes a man with a cart containing flowers."

"Right," agreed Martelli. "And now the other two men are opening the casket, making final adjustments to the lining and the corpse's hands, straightening out the lining around the deceased's shoes—by the way, never look down there, Missy . . . it's where the viscera bag is stored—and so forth. Nothing appears to be out of the ordinary."

"I agree . . . looks like business as usual."

Martelli and Dugan watched the screen in silence as the men went about their work.

Finally, Missy spoke. "Okay, looks like everything's ready. See? The men are leaving the sanctuary."

The date-time display on the screen showed a time of 12:34 pm.

"They're probably going outside to grab a sandwich or smoke, Lou. Note that no one is in the camera's field of view. I checked all of the other cameras as well. There's not a person in the sanctuary at this time. But then—"

"Wait! What's that in the corner, Missy?"

Missy started to laugh. "That, my friend, is the shooter."

The screen showed someone who appeared to be a man entering the large, raised platform that stretched across the front of the church and upon which the altar stood. Dressed in a long priest's robe and wearing a black, low-crowned, wide-brimmed ecclesiastical hat, he emerged slowly from behind the curtains at the far, left back of the platform, as one viewed the sanctuary from the rear. After looking around to ensure no one was in the sanctuary, he walked down the stairs, and at the bottom, turned left and quickly made his way toward the casket.

"I can't see his face, Missy! Where the hell did he come from?"

"I checked some of our surveillance cameras on the streets around the church. One caught a shot of him walking into the small cemetery behind the building and entering through the service entrance. But that's about all I can tell you. Now, watch closely."

The shooter stopped at the casket, turned to see if anyone was watching, took something out of his pocket and placed it into the corpse's mouth.

"That must have been the garlic, Lou."

"Right, and now he's screwing the silencer onto the gun barrel."

"I see that."

They watched as the shooter pushed the silencer against the side of the casket and pulled the trigger.

Martelli shook his head. "Bada-bing bada-boom, right through the casket into the corpse."

They continued watching intently as the shooter retraced his footsteps across the sanctuary floor, climbed the stairs to the platform, and continued through the curtains to make his escape, most probably using the same service entrance through which he had entered.

"Were you able to track him on his way off the church's property?"

"Not very far. We don't have a lot of cameras in that area. And to make things worse, at some point he probably shed the priest's garb and either stuck it in a bag or dumped it."

"Okay, go back and grab the best screen shot of the shooter you can get and e-mail it to CSU."

"10-4."

Martelli reached for the phone on Dugan's workbench and dialed the Department's Crime Scene Unit.

"NYPD CSU, Sergeant Reynolds."

"Reynolds, this is Martelli of the First."

"Hey, Lou, long time no see. How are you and the family?"

"Good, Adam. And you and yours?"

"Great. How can I help you?"

"We had a shooting yesterday at a church in the First. Some guy pumped a round into a corpse."

"I know. What the hell is that all about?"

"Beats the shit out of me."

"Man, it's getting weird out there, Lou."

"Tell me about it. Listen, Dugan is e-mailing you a screen shot of the shooter. It's not great, but it's the best we have. The perp—and we're assuming it's a man—disguised himself as a priest. He was dressed in a long robe and wore a black, low-crowned, wide-brimmed ecclesiastical hat."

"Okay."

"Could you send a CSU team back to the church to search for additional evidence? Perhaps your people'll be able to lift a print or two from the inside and outside knobs of the door at the service entrance. Or, in showing the screen shot to people in the neighborhood, maybe they'll find someone who can tell them in which direction he walked. In the best of all worlds, we might even get a better description of the person or an ID, but I doubt it."

"I'll take care of it, Lou. Are you considering putting out a BOLO for the guy?"

"No. We don't have enough information to go on yet. And the guy isn't going to be walking around in that get-up, that's for sure. All we need is for our people to be questioning every man of the cloth they encounter on the street, and we'll have the Catholic Church all over us. If that happens, you know the media . . . they'll blow the whole thing way out of proportion."

"Like they do everything else."

"Right. That would make our job even more difficult than it already is."

"Yeah, I know what you mean. Used to be you could trust them, but today, most are just out to make a quick name for themselves. Anyway, I'll send a unit to the church now."

"Thanks, Adam. I owe you!"

"Don't mention it, Lou."

Martelli returned the handset to its cradle and turned his attention back to Dugan.

"Okay, Missy, did Antonetti have anything else to say?"

"Yeah, he said to tell you to stop at the Korean grocer's on your way home tonight, buy some garlic, and hang it around your neck. He said you can't be too careful these days, especially when there might be vampires prowling Gotham City at night."

"Well isn't he just a barrel of laughs! Listen, NYPD needs this case like a hole in the head . . . chasing what someone wants the Department to think is the 'killer' of vampires, werewolves, and other forms of lowlife."

Missy could barely stifle a grin. "Don't you mean 'no-life,' Martelli?"

Despite himself, Martelli had to laugh. "Give me a break, will ya?

"What else did the 'court jester' have to say?"

"Actually, he said he wanted to see you this morning after you're done here. Even though there had been a cursory autopsy performed on the deceased at the time of his death, something important turned up."

"What was it?"

"He wouldn't tell me . . . he just said he wanted to see you when we finished here."

■ *Theodore Jerome Cohen*

<u>Three</u>

Deputy Coroner Michael Antonetti had already been at work for more than two hours by the time Martelli walked into the morgue, which was located in the basement of Police Plaza One. Now, standing over the corpse that had been brought from the church the previous afternoon, Antonetti was again reviewing the toxicology report he had received that morning.

"Michael, Missy said you wanted to see me. She said you found something."

"Louis, thank you for coming down. Yes, I found something important."

"What's that?"

"Well, the official cause of death of the man who was supposed to be buried yesterday—his name, by the way, was Phillip Weston—was acute myocardial infarction, more commonly known as a heart attack. This determination was based on an autopsy performed by a coroner upstate, where the man died."

"Didn't he die here, in the city?"

"Heaven's no. He passed away in his summer home up north . . . at Lake George.

"Anyway, the local coroner didn't suspect anything unusual. The deceased was 76 years old and according to his doctor up there, Susan Allerton, he had a history of high blood pressure. I know, because I talked with her early this morning."

"How could she release Weston's medical history to you, Michael? Even in death, HIPAA protects his privacy."

"True, but I called Weston's daughter last night. She faxed permission to the clinic at Lake George, requesting that Dr. Allerton cooperate with the police in their investigation of her father's death. Call the doctor if you like. She'll talk to you. Here's her number."

He handed a piece of notepaper to Martelli. "So," continued Antonetti, "not suspecting anything out of the ordinary, the local coroner did a cursory examination, signed the death certificate, and released the body to the daughter. She had the body brought back to city by representatives from the funeral home based in Manhattan for burial under the terms of the contract the deceased had executed years ago with that establishment."

"Okay, I follow you. So, what is it that *you* uncovered?"

"Well, you know me, Louis. People normally don't go around stuffing garlic in other people's mouths . . . unless they're Italian, of course. And moreover, they certainly don't go around pumping slugs into embalmed corpses unless—"

"Unless, for some perverse reason, there's unfinished business that needs to be addressed . . . or a score settled."

"Precisely! So, I got to thinking. Just how did our Mr. Weston *really* die? Might he have had some help meeting his Maker?"

"And after having our lab run an extensive set of toxicology tests, you learned—"

"He was murdered. And it was, as Agatha Christie would say, a murder most foul. In fact, I almost missed it but for the fact that I fortuitously decided to request the entire gamut of toxicology tests, including several that look for some of the more exotic poisons."

"*Exotic* poisons?"

"Yes, and more specifically, snake venoms. You know, they work in two ways. First, there are neurotoxins, which disable the victim's central nervous system, causing the prey's muscles to stop working. Basically, the victim suffocates to death.

"Then, there are hemotoxins, which target the circulatory system. These toxins break down clotting compounds in blood, causing uncontrolled bleeding."

"Ugly stuff, Michael."

"To be sure. There are roughly three hundred species of venomous snakes, so testing for their venom is an enormous chore. But I asked the lab to put a rush on it yesterday afternoon."

Martelli stroked his chin. "And I take it the tests came back positive."

"Ooooh, yes. And the toxin found is a doozy! Your killer used a neurotoxin . . . specifically, the neurotoxic venom from a Philippine Cobra. That's what killed Weston! Death usually comes in as little as 30 minutes.

"By the way, I can't rule out the possibility that in addition to having suffered respiratory failure, Weston also may have suffered a heart attack. This wouldn't be unusual under the circumstances for a man his age."

"I understand, Michael."

"Mind you, Louis, after everything Weston's body's been through since his death, the level of poison anywhere in his remains is extremely low. But I gave the lab three different samples cut from different parts of the body. Two of the three confirmed the presence of Philippine Cobra neurotoxic venom."

15

Martelli thought for a moment.

"So, Michael, now we have a murder on our hands, committed either by the party who abused the corpse yesterday afternoon—"

"Or a third party, who may or may not be working with yesterday's shooter."

Martelli clasped his hands on top of his head and pushed it down until his chin touched his chest. "Dammit! This couldn't be a nice clean first-degree murder! It's always something new and different in this damn city!"

"Can I use your phone?"

"Knock yourself out."

Martelli picked up the handset on Antonetti's console and dialed the number for his partner, Detective-Specialist Sean O'Keeffe.

"Yes, Michael, how can I help you?"

"Sean, it's me . . . Lou."

"Oh, I'm sorry, Lou. I saw Antonetti's name come up on Caller ID."

"Not to worry. Listen, we have a problem. The shooting yesterday in the church—"

"You mean the one where some guy pumped a slug into a corpse?"

"Yeah, one and the same. Turns out that the guy in the casket didn't die a natural death. He was murdered upstate, in the Lake George area. They didn't catch it up there in the autopsy because some exotic snake venom had been used to stop the vic's heart. The coroner never suspected anything except death by natural causes. To him, it looked as if the guy suffered a coronary."

"Interesting. So, how can I help you?"

"The vic's name was Phillip Weston. Find out where he lived down here. We're going to have to toss his place."

"Got it."

"Also, contact the sheriff's department in Lake George. Ask the sheriff if they could to tape off Weston's summer home, mark it as a crime scene, and post someone on the property around the clock until we can drive up there and go through the place for evidence. It would also be nice—and please, be as diplomatic as possible when you broach this subject—if they waited until we got there before entering the house. Then, we'll toss the place together. I'm sure they'll cooperate, but we do need to ask."

"I understand."

"And be sure to tell them that we'll be more than happy to give them all of the credit for whatever comes out of our joint efforts . . . that this is not about the NYPD taking credit for solving the case but rather, about making them heroes!"

"You bet, Lou."

"Good. Then, once you locate the guy's apartment, get a search warrant and hop over there. Take a black and white with you. Let me know where you are once you get there. Tape off the apartment and start going through it. I'll join you as soon as I can. There must be something over there or in his place on Lake George that'll lead us to his murderer."

"Okay. So, ah, what are your plans?"

"I have something to clear up here while I wait for your call."

"I'll be in touch."

"Bye."

Martelli turned his attention back to the deputy coroner.

"Michael, given this turn of events, I want to ask you something."

"And that would be?"

"When I was with Missy earlier, she said the slug you pulled from the corpse matched one pulled from a vic a year ago. Here's the file."

Antonetti took the file and opened it. "Hmmm . . . Byron Hayes. Our man Eastman did the autopsy on him. Good man, Eastman. Very thorough. Let's see . . . he ran the usual suite of tox screenings . . . nothing exhaustive like the set I just ran, but then, there was no suggestion they were required. Hayes was shot once in the heart and apparently died instantly in Riverside Park, the victim of a robbery gone bad. At least that's the way it seemed at the time."

"But what if the two murders are connected by more than the use of the same firearm, Michael? What if Weston and Hayes knew their killer—hell, perhaps all three men knew each other. If so, what was the nature of that relationship? And why would someone go to the trouble of stuffing garlic in Weston's mouth and then, pump a slug into his corpse?"

"I don't know the answers to those questions, Louis, but I think I know what you're about to ask me to do."

"You bet! Get a court order to exhume Hayes's body. I'll wager a month's pay you'll find garlic in his mouth. And unless I miss my guess, I think you'll find the body or the casket was desecrated in some other way as well."

Four

It was late-morning when O'Keeffe called Martelli from Weston's apartment on West End Avenue. "We've got the apartment sealed off, Lou. I just texted you the address and apartment number."

"Got it, Sean. Thanks. I'm on my way. Does the place look disturbed in any way?"

"No. And I talked with the super. He said as far as he could tell, no one's been in the apartment since Weston died. He got a call from the daughter this morning, though. She had told him she was going to start packing and moving her father's belongings today and then, clean the apartment in a few days so she could show it to prospective buyers. But now that the police are holding her father's body indefinitely, she said she was going to delay doing anything until her father is buried."

"Okay, make sure the back entrance is locked and keep a uniformed officer at the front entrance. I don't want anyone, and that includes the super and the daughter, going into the apartment until we've finished collecting evidence."

"Got it."

"I'm on my way."

It took Martelli 25 minutes to reach Weston's apartment. O'Keeffe was waiting for him.

"Did you find anything?"

"Not much. The guy lived a Spartan existence, that's for sure. We did locate his personal computer, and I've boxed it for shipment to the Evidence Room."

"Great. Anything else?"

"Just copies of a few recent e-mails, monthly checking and savings account statements, cancelled checks, checkbooks, utility bills, and the like, and some calendars— you know, monthly planners for several years . . . 2006, '07, '08, '09, and '10."

"Perhaps the calendar for 2011 is up north."

"Could be, Lou. Anyway, I'll get all of this back to the Evidence Room."

"Good. Anything else?"

"Oh, yes. I went through his library in the living room. He apparently read quite a bit . . . lots of mystery thrillers, murder mysteries, and the like. What's interesting, however, is that several of the books and volumes of bound documents stored on the top shelf were, well . . ."

"Well, what?"

"On the subject of vampires."

"You know, my daughter, Tiffany, seems to be talking a lot about vampires these days. Apparently they're all the rage with teenagers, even some adults, with new books and movies coming out every week. What kinds of books and documents did you find?"

"They're not what teenagers are reading, that's for sure. Take a look for yourself."

O'Keeffe led him to the bookshelf and pulled down a first edition of *Vampires, Burial, and Death: Folklore and Reality* by Paul Barber.

Martelli started paging through the volume. "Okay, the guy appears to have an intense interest in this subject. The book is even autographed by the author. Let's see what else is up here."

Martelli pulled down two more volumes, both autographed by the authors as well. The first was a copy of *The Vampire Encyclopedia* by Matthew Bunson. The second was Alan Dundes's *The Vampire: A Casebook* published by the University of Wisconsin Press. Several other vampire-related books appeared to have been borrowed from the New York Public Library. Many were long overdue. Martelli chuckled to himself. *Well, I guess they're going to have something of a problem collecting the fines on these,* he thought.

Martelli turned to O'Keeffe. "At the least, Weston was a serious collector of this kind of material, I'll say that." He pulled on the lobe of his right ear while he thought for a few seconds. "You have to wonder if, in his mind, he didn't take it *so* seriously that maybe . . . and mind you, I'm just thinking out loud . . . he had a deal with someone such that after he died—regardless of how he died—the other person would put garlic into his mouth and shoot a bullet into his corpse."

"But why?"

Martelli threw his hands into the air. "Hell, I don't know! Maybe he was so immersed in this stuff that he thought of himself as a vampire and believed that this was the thing to do . . . one last act, to make sure he never rose from the grave."

"Man, if that's the case, this guy must have been loony tunes!"

"Ya think?"

They laughed. "Pack up his books and take them to the Evidence Room. There's too much here to go through it now.

"And by the way, what happened when you called the sheriff in Lake George?"

"Oh, yeah . . . I almost forgot. Nice guy, really nice. Geoffrey Ward's his name. His family's lived in the area since the early 1900s. He was surprised by what I told him. And he also was very appreciative of the fact that we'd not only help him solve Weston's murder but also, see to it that he got the credit. Apparently he's facing re-election, so he can use all the help we can give him.

"He said he'd send a deputy over to Weston's place on the lake and seal off the house so no one could enter it until we got there. When do you think we should go, Lou?"

"Tomorrow morning. I'll call Weston's daughter when I get back to the office, explain to her what's happening—to the extent I can—and make arrangements to pick up a key for the lake house."

"What about questioning the funeral home personnel, Weston's family members, and the other mourners?"

"I already requested that Eddy Lewis and Mary Fitzpatrick be assigned those duties. The captain agreed."

"Good move."

"Okay, Sean, help me find some boxes for these books, and we can be on our way. And remind me to leave word on the way out that this apartment must remain sealed until further notice. You never know . . . we might need to return."

Five

Tiffany Martelli had no sooner come to the breakfast table when her father put down his *New York Times* and turned to her. "Honey, what is the fascination teenagers have with vampires these days?"

Rob, Tiffany's younger brother, perked up. He had a look of genuine pleasure on his face, as if he were about to see his sister made to look like a fool. Even Stephanie stopped pouring Tiffany's cereal into her bowl and looked at her husband quizzically.

"Like, you're not serious, are you, Dad?"

"I'm dead serious, no pun intended."

No one said anything.

"Okay, look, honey . . . I have this case. It involves someone who is going around stuffing garlic in the mouths of corpses."

Tiffany twisted her face in a knot. "Ewww . . . gross! How can you talk about things like that at the table, Dad?"

Great, thought Stephanie. *Now Lou will start having nightmares about vampires coming after him.*

After Martelli returned home from Walter Reed National Military Medical Center following his release from the Army, he was plagued by nightmares. Night after night Stephanie was awakened by his screams . . . screams of a desperate man yelling to the pilot and copilot of their ill-fated Black

23

Hawk helicopter, urging them to free themselves from the debris in the cockpit and fight their way back through the flames to the rear sliding door, where he stood waiting for them. She knew that when he saw they could not get out of the cockpit, and despite his shattered left leg and second-degree burns on his hip, that he had fought his way to the front of the aircraft, only to be driven back by the intense heat from fuel that had ignited.

Months after he returned home, he finally was able to tell her that his last memory before blacking out was of the cries from the cockpit . . . desperate cries for help that he never was able to answer . . . dreadful cries that he heard over and over again in his nightmares until he thought he would go insane.

It was Stephanie who was always there when that happened, soothing him, changing the bed sheets that had become drenched in sweat, and assuring him that 'this, too, shall pass' and tomorrow would be a better day.

Rob went back to eating his breakfast. Clearly, this conversation would not yield the result he had in mind.

"I know it's a bit, shall we say, unusual—"

"Unusual? Dad! Seriously, have you thought of, like, finding another job? I can't believe the creeps you have to deal with."

"No argument there, honey. But I need to get inside this perp's head. I need to understand what's making him tick. Why would someone do this?

"So again, what is the fascination people in your crowd have with vampires? I mean, I see all these advertisements for the *Twilight Saga* films . . . movies like *Eclipse*. What's that all about?"

Stephanie broke in. "Let me help your poor father understand, dear.

24

"Look, Lou, teenagers are curious about things they don't understand. When we were kids, we had a fascination with extraterrestrials. Remember all those movies and television shows we used to watch on the subject. Today, kids, both gals *and* guys, are interested in the supernatural. And then, especially for girls, there's that whole thing about forbidden love . . . you know, the 'Romeo and Juliet' love story. I know it's more complex than that, but still, perhaps that will help you understand a little better what's going on."

"It does . . . in the case of teenagers. But what about adults? What's the attraction there?"

Tiffany put down her spoon and wiped her mouth with a napkin. "Well, there is one thing my boyfriend, Jeff, mentioned a few weeks ago."

Rob looked up and muttered under his breath. "Ah, yes, lover boy!"

Three pair of eyes burned a hole in his forehead.

"That's not necessary, Rob," his mother admonished.

Martelli gently placed his left hand on his daughter's right arm. "Please go on, Tiffany. Believe me when I tell you, this could be very helpful to me and the Department."

"Well, Jeffrey said he had seen a rerun of a *CSI: Las Vegas* episode a few weeks ago. It showed CSI officers in a place called a 'blood bar' or something like that, talking to a man who drank other peoples' blood. Jeff said he really liked the name of the man."

"Do you remember the name?"

"I think he said it was 'Lazarus Caine,' or something like that."

Martelli's smiled. "I'm liking this Jeff Romano more and more with every passing minute. You know, Tiffany, in the Bible, Jesus raised Lazarus from the dead in the city of

Bethany, so the man's name has some interesting connotations."

Stephanie had a look of amusement on her face. "Why, Louis Martelli, you surprise me. And here, my parents thought all along that the reason I married you was because you were such an gorgeous hunk!"

"Oh, give me a break," moaned Rob, "can't you see I'm eating!"

Martelli laughed. "Tell me, Tiffany, what else did Jeff tell you about vampires?"

"Well, after we saw one of the latest vampire movies a few weeks ago, we were, like, sitting in his parent's den—"

Stephanie's eyes shot wide open. "You were what?"

"Aw, Mom, give me a break! His parents were home, watching television on the other side of the room."

Stephanie looked at her husband out of the corner of her eye and breathed a sigh of relief.

"Anyway, we did an Internet search on the subject of vampires. Did you know that the Persians were, like, one of the first to depict blood-drinking demons?"

Martelli and his wife looked at their daughter as if she had just been awarded the Nobel Prize in Literature.

"And then, there are tales of the mythical Lilitu, which gave rise to the Hebrew Lilith and her daughters, the Lilu, from Hebrew demonology."

Stephanie's had a look of disbelief on her face. *Is this my daughter speaking?*

"I didn't know that," commented Martelli, his interest piqued.

"And," continued Tiffany, "Lilitu, who was considered a demon, was often depicted as living on the blood of babies. Like, maybe the guy you're chasing is into stuff like that, Dad!"

26

"God, I hope not, honey." *I pray not!* thought Martelli.

Tiffany look worried. "Well, there are some strange people out there, Dad, and I really need you to be careful. I don't want you coming home looking like you did after that one case . . . you know, all beat up after your 'best friend' from high school worked you over in the basement of that guy's home in the Hamptons!"

She was talking, of course, about the case involving Islamic terrorists who used a front organization in Brooklyn to launder money, with the funds subsequently used to purchase weapons for jihadi movements in the Middle East.

"Tiffany, first, I'll be *very* careful. I promise. Second, thank you for the quick lesson on vampires. You can't begin to know how much help you—"

The blare of his partner's car horn, signaling it was time to leave for Lake George, interrupted him. Martelli gulped down the last few drops of coffee in his mug, threw on his suit coat, kissed everyone goodbye, and grabbing his briefcase, walked, with a slight limp, through the front door, down the steps, and to the street to where O'Keeffe was waiting at the curb in his unmarked *Crown Vic*.

■ *Theodore Jerome Cohen*

<u>Six</u>

'**G**ood morning, Lou. Man, it'll be great to get out of the city and into upstate New York. I can't wait to hit the open road and get started on this case."

"You and me, both, Sean. The last two days have been a nightmare. Of all things . . . some guy dressed as a priest enters a Catholic church just before a funeral service is scheduled to begin, pumps a round into the deceased's corpse using the same gun that had been used to kill another man in the city a year earlier, only for us to learn that the man about to be buried had been murdered several days earlier using snake venom."

Sean laughed. "Captain Hanlon assigns us all the easy cases."

"Ain't that the truth! Oh, by the way, I asked Antonetti to get a court order and exhume the body of the guy who was shot down a year ago on the Upper West Side."

Sean nodded. "That would have been my next move."

"I'm thinking both men must have pissed off the same shooter . . . at least there's a good chance it's the same shooter. And if it is, there's probably a good chance, as well, that all three knew each other. That's what I'm banking on. The guy killed in the Riverside Park was shot in the heart . . . not in the chest, or the head, or the stomach, but directly in the heart. I think the shooter had more on his mind than just

29

killing the vic. I think he wanted to make sure he never rose from the grave."

"What the hell are you smoking, Martelli, and why aren't you sharing it?"

"You can laugh, my friend, but before this case is over, I have a hunch we're both going to see a side of life—and death—we never dreamed existed."

"Did Lewis and Fitzpatrick learn anything from the mourners at Weston's funeral, Lou?"

"No, that whole exercise turned out to be a dry hole. No one saw anything or could provide useful information."

"More the rule than the exception in our business, that's for sure."

O'Keeffe fought his way through the heavy morning rush hour traffic. In 45 minutes he emerged north of the metropolitan area and merged onto I-87 North. "It's going to take us at another three and a half hours to get there, depending on traffic, but at least it's a straight shot. Just let me know anytime you want to get out and stretch, and we'll stop."

"Go for it. Steph packed some things for us to munch on while we're on the road. I have them in my briefcase."

"Great. I've got soft drinks in a cooler on the floor behind me. We can stop for lunch in Albany. I know a great little diner just off the Interstate."

Within an hour the traffic thinned considerably, and the men started to make good time. Their conversation roamed over a variety of subjects, ranging from current, to cold, to closed cases. Their exchanges were 'all business.' There was no idle chatter, no vetting of rumors. And for good reason. O'Keeffe was not known to make small talk.

They had worked as a team for three years, but rarely met for purely social reasons other than at events sponsored by the Department. If they knew anything about each other and their private lives, they had picked it up in bits and pieces, usually in snippets conveyed, for example, in anecdotes much like events captured in the photographs found in picture albums.

Unlike O'Keeffe, however, Martelli enjoyed chatting . . . even sparring verbally, especially with Dugan and Alexa Lindsay Beauvais, an NYPD senior forensic financial analyst. And when bored, he often attempted to see what mischief he could create, especially if it offered the possibility of jerking his partner's chain.

"Hey, look at the car in front of us . . . it looks like no one's driving."

To be sure, there was a driver. But all the men could see was the back of the driver's headrest.

"Hit the lights and siren, Sean. Pull him over and cite him for DWS."

"DWS? What the hell's that?"

"Driving while short!"

Martelli was laughing so hard he had tears rolling down his cheeks.

"Oh, that's funny, Lou, really funny. And not very PC, I might add.

"Speaking of things PC, Dugan's going to file a sexual harassment complaint against you one of these days if you're not careful for the way you talk to her."

"Dugan? Are you kidding? She told me last year she *grades* sexual harassment."

"Oh, yeah, so how are you doing?"

Martelli stopped laughing. "Not very well, I'm afraid . . . 'B minus,' she said."

Now it was Sean's turn to laugh. "She's got your number."

Shortly after 9 AM, Martelli took out his cell phone. "I think I'll give our Weston's doctor in Lake George a call. She was the last one to examine him prior to his death and is in the best position to speak to his general health at the time."

He dialed the number Antonetti had given to him and heard two rings.

"Dr. Allerton's office, Marge speaking."

"Marge, this is Detective Louis Martelli, New York Police Department. By any chance, would Dr. Allerton have a few minutes to speak with me?"

"Just a moment, Detective . . . I think she's between patients. Let me see if I can catch her. I'm going to put you on hold, and either she or I'll be right back."

"Thanks, Marge."

Martelli turned toward Sean to let him know what was happening. "She's checking to see if she's available—"

"Good morning, Detective Martelli, this is Susan Allerton. Dr. Antonetti said you might be calling."

"Good morning, Doctor. Thanks for taking my call. I promise not to take too much of your time, but as you know, we have a bit of a problem on our hands."

"Oh my, yes. I understand dear Mr. Weston was murdered. Our coroner is kicking himself for missing that—"

"Well, he mustn't do that. If Deputy Coroner Antonetti didn't have access to the lab he uses, and if he hadn't submitted three samples for some pretty exhaustive tox screening, we wouldn't be having this conversation, I can assure you of that. Please pass that along to your coroner."

"You're most kind, Detective."

"Please, call me Lou."

"All right, Lou . . . my friends call me Susan."

"You were Mr. Weston's personal physician, correct?"

"Well, yes, but only during the so-called 'summer season.' He used to come up here in late April or early May, and stay until late October. Then he would move back to his apartment in Manhattan. I think he used Dr. Myers in the city . . . Dr. Glenn J. Myers."

"And would you say that other than high blood pressure, Mr. Weston was in good health?"

"Yes, I'd say he was in generally good health for a man his age. He had borderline hypertension, but we had that under control using a very low dose of losartan potassium. And though he had suffered from migraines earlier in his life, they had abated over the last five years to the point where he only needed to take one sumatriptan tablet now and then to stop the pain."

"I see. So, may I conclude, then, you didn't notice any changes in his general health over the last few years that seemed, shall we say, the least bit unusual?"

"Well, now that you mention it, two or three times during the last five years, when he came in for his spring checkup— he usually saw me right after he arrived for the summer—his CBC—"

"What's that?"

"Complete blood count . . . his complete blood count showed him to be slightly anemic. I also observed several hematomas on his arms."

"Hematomas?"

"Bruises."

"How might an individual get one of those, Susan?"

"Well, if a needle is inserted in such a way that it slips through a vein, it can cause local bleeding under the skin, resulting in a bruise."

"I see."

"I asked him how he got them, and he said he had recently donated blood. So, I suggested he keep the areas clean and take iron supplements to build his red blood cell count back to acceptable levels."

"Did he seem nervous when you mentioned the fact that his blood tests showed him to be anemic or when you brought up the subject of the bruises?"

"No, we simply discussed it and moved on. It didn't seem to faze him."

"Did he ever give you an indication he was troubled or worried about anything in his life . . . that something might be bothering him?"

"No, I can't say he did. He always seemed relaxed when he came to the office . . . happy that winter was over and looking forward to enjoying summer at the lake. So, no, I'd have to say I saw no signs that would indicate he was worried about anything."

"Okay, one more thing—"

"Yes?"

"Do you think it might be possible to have your receptionist make a copy of Weston's medical records for us? We're heading to Lake George now. Perhaps we could stop by your office on our way into town and pick them up? You never know, there might be something in them that could prove important to our investigation."

"I'll have them waiting for you, Detective. My office is on the west side of East Shore Drive, near the A&W Restaurant. You can't miss it . . . there's a big sign out front."

"That's great. Well, look, you've been most kind, and I'm sure you have patients waiting. We'll be by sometime in the next few hours. And if you think of anything that might be of help to us, don't hesitate to call Dr. Antonetti or me, anytime, day or night."

"I'll do that, Lou."

"Thanks, Susan. It was nice speaking with you."

"Take care."

Sean, who was not able to hear everything that the doctor had said, looked over at his partner. "What was that all about?"

"I'm not sure. She said that there were times when Weston's blood tests came back showing he was slightly anemic. Not only that, she said he occasionally had bruises on his arm that looked as if they had resulted from needles having been inserted improperly."

"Hell, I've had those. Sometimes a nurse who is preparing to draw blood doesn't hit the sweet spot just right, and the area where the needle was inserted will be black and blue for a week."

"Yeah, but she said this happened a few times over a period of five years. The excuse Weston always gave was that he had given blood. Let's see if that checks out."

Martelli speed dialed Antonetti. It took a few seconds for the connection to be made.

"Louis, what's happening?"

"Michael, I just spoke with Dr. Allerton. Nice lady."

"Yes, she is."

"She said that on few visits to her office, Weston showed signs of anemia and had bruises on his arms. Weston explained that he had just given blood. So, she simply suggested that he keep the areas clean and take iron supplements to bring his red blood cell count up."

"But you suspect something else, don't you?"

"It would be easier if we found fang marks on his neck . . . yes, dammit, I suspect something else."

The three men laughed.

35

"Look, Michael, do me a favor. Develop a list of the service providers in the greater New York City area—you know, people like the Red Cross—who draw blood. Send the list to Sergeant Reynolds at CSU. Ask him if he can find out whether Phillip Weston donated blood any time in the last five years. I'm not quite sure how Reynolds is going to get that information because of privacy issues, but if anyone can do it, he can."

"I understand. It's going to be difficult, all right, but let's see what he can do. I'll start preparing the list now."

"Thanks, pal. And by the way, if you don't mind, could you take a few minutes and call Weston's other doctor—let me see . . . oh yes, Dr. Glenn J. Myers—and see if you get the same story. You know, mild anemia, bruises on the arms, blood donations, and the like? Poke around, gentle like."

"I'll do that."

"Thanks, Michael. You know how to reach me."

"Safe travels, Lou."

Sean shook his head. "So, do you think this guy Weston was into drinking blood?"

"Damned if I know. But at the least, it's highly likely that someone was drinking *his*."

"What a crazy world this is."

<u>Seven</u>

Following a quick lunch in a diner outside Albany, the team hit the road again. Sean did the driving. Not that Martelli did not offer to take the wheel several times.

"I don't mind driving, Lou. Frankly, after being stuck in city traffic almost every day of my life, it's a pleasure to let this baby 'run' at 80 to 90 miles per hour. It might even do her some good."

He chuckled. "I put some additive in the gas tank before we left. By the time we return, I should be getting ten percent better gas mileage than when we started. Just don't tell the guys in the Motor Pool. They'll jump all over me for not carrying a union card!"

Martelli laughed. "Don't get my wife started on the subject of unions. She's had more than her fair share of problems with them. She even caught a union guy 'punching out' a friend's timecard last year so the friend could claim overtime he didn't work. It was on a job for the US government. That little trick cost both union men their jobs, and their employer—or should I say their former employer— was put on probation by the feds for truth-in-timecard violations. One more violation and that company will be barred from bidding on future federal contracts for several years."

"Wow, your wife sounds like one tough lady! She doesn't fool around, does she?"

"Not when someone messes with her dinner plate. If the government auditors had detected that violation, both the subcontractor cited *and* Steph's company would have been written up."

"You know, you're a lucky man, Lou. Beautiful wife, two great kids, nice home life . . . ." O'Keeffe's voice trailed off as he drifted into his own world.

Martelli watched him out of the corner of his eye, saying nothing. His partner was just under 6 feet tall, of medium build, and weighed in at a lean 170 pounds. Blond with blue eyes, he tanned easily to a dark bronze, which, Martelli had heard, caught many a lady's eye during the occasional summer weekend or holiday he spent at the Jersey Shore . . . that is, when he had time to break away from his and Martelli's heavy caseload.

Martelli knew that marathons were O'Keeffe's passion. There was no major race in the New York metropolitan area that had been held during the last three years, including the ING New York City Marathon, in which his partner did not finish in the top fifty.

Though they had been partners for more than three years, O'Keeffe knew far more about Martelli than Martelli knew about O'Keeffe. Which was not surprising, given Martelli's gregarious nature. O'Keeffe, on the other hand, was far more private. And though not one given to idle chatter, there were times when O'Keeffe completely blindsided people by the sheer audacity of this creative repartee. That said, however, he was not loquacious. He would simply say what he had to say, and that was that.

Over their years working together, Martelli had been able to piece a few things together from their conversations. For example, he knew that his partner grew up in the Midwest, Wisconsin, to be exact, the son of traveling salesman—farm

38

machinery was his line—and a stay-at-home mother. His father was on the road three weeks out of four, and in his absence, O'Keeffe's mother took up with a steady stream of lovers.

When O'Keeffe's father came home early one Friday afternoon and caught his wife in bed with another man, he threw her out of the house. Tragically, O'Keeffe's mother and her lover died a week later in a collision on a rain-slicked road near Sun Prairie, WI. By that time, however, O'Keeffe had already been sent to live with his father's sister in Appleton, WI, where he stayed until he finished high school.

College wasn't an option with money being tight, so O'Keeffe enlisted in the Army and fortuitously, found a 'home' in the MPs. Following graduation from the US Army Military Police School at Fort Leonard Wood, MO, he did two tours in Iraq before returning home. In civilian life, he put his military training to good use as a police officer in a small New England town. And thanks to the GI Bill, he earned a bachelor's degree in Law Enforcement from the nearby state university. Following graduation, and upon meeting the NYPD's requirements for Detective-Specialist, O'Keeffe joined the New York Police Department.

Martelli chuckled. *Not a hellava lot in the way of information to show for three years on the job together,* he thought. Not once in all that time did O'Keeffe mention if he ever had been married or even had a 'special lady.' And though Martelli was not one to pry when it came to personal matters, every now and then when he, Stephanie, Sean, and Sean's date were together at an NYPD-sponsored function, Stephanie would 'poke around' where angels feared to tread.

O'Keeffe never failed to arrive at the annual Christmas party sponsored by the First Precinct with a beautiful woman on his arm. But he never was seen with the same woman twice. And though he was quite the dancer, he rarely mentioned an evening's festivities once the celebration was over.

Martelli often thought what O'Keeffe witnessed between his father and mother must have had a debilitating effect on the man's ability to establish long-term relationships with women. *I guess Nature's mold sets early,* he mused one day while thinking about his partner. *Maybe O'Keeffe knows instinctively that for someone to be married to a police officer is not the easiest way to live. Maybe this is the reason he shies away from anything even resembling a serious relationship with a woman.*

Martelli had to know better than most how much of a toll the job of a police officer can take on a marriage. As a detective in a large city, he often was away from his family for 48, 60, and even 72 hours at a stretch, week after week. To say it made life difficult was an understatement. Throw in a wife who worked full time and two teenagers, and the scene was set for marital disaster.

And the stress! On the job, he never knew who, or what, was waiting for him around the next corner.

But it was worse for his wife . . . *for any officer's wife.* She never knew if a knock on the door announced the Chaplain, there to extend the Department's deepest condolences on the death of her husband and her children's father in the line of duty.

That is how it was for Martelli's mother when the Department Chaplain came to their home and told her—at a time when Martelli was in the Army and could not be there to comfort her—that Pietro, her husband, had died in a hail of bullets from the guns of two escaped felons he had tracked to, and mortally wounded in, a warehouse on the docks in lower Manhattan.

The funeral procession that followed his father's casket to the cemetery in Brooklyn included more than 300 patrol cars from 17 states as far away as Florida to the south and Kansas to the west.

It was small comfort. His mother never was the same after that. Many who knew her said they saw the light go out of her eyes when the last shovelful of dirt was spread on Pietro's grave.

Who can blame O'Keeffe, thought Martelli, *if he chooses to play a lone hand in life?*

"You've been awful quiet, Lou. Problems at home?"

Martelli chuckled. "Just thinking back to the great time we had at the last Christmas party. I really do like kicking back for a few hours during the holidays . . . you know, spending a little time with Steph and the kids . . . just getting away from the job."

"Yeah, it's always fun. And man, can your wife dance. She left me out of breath last year on that one song. What the hell was it? Oh, yeah . . . *Shout.* I can't believe that song has been around for more than 50 years."

"Thanks for keeping her busy for a few minutes. If she had dragged me onto the dance floor for that one, I would have ended up having to have my *other* leg fitted for a prosthetic device!"

"Man, you're something else. You lost a leg in Iraq, and you just keep charging ahead as if nothing's changed."

"It hasn't, really. I'm still the same guy I always was, thanks to Steph. You know, we've known each other since high school. We were inseparable then, and we're inseparable now. If it wasn't for her, I don't think I would have made it when I got home from Iraq. It got pretty rough there, for a while, and—"

41

Martelli's cell phone started ringing. He could tell from the ringtone that it was Antonetti.

"Yes, Michael."

"Lou, I talked with Dr. Myers. He gave me the same story you heard from Dr. Allerton. He said that over the last several years, Weston would present with anemia and bruises. When Myers questioned him, Weston said he had donated blood."

"What did he do about it?"

"Nothing. He couldn't very well accuse his patient of lying without losing him. And frankly, slight anemia and bruising are not life-threatening."

"Okay, so Weston was up to something. Someone was drawing his blood, but who? Any word yet from Reynolds at CSU?"

"No. He said it might take a day or two for him to work his contacts. But he assured me that if Weston had donated blood in the State of New York, he'd be able to confirm the locations, dates, and times. 'Hell,' he said, 'I'll tell you who stuck him.'"

"It doesn't get any better than that, Michael. You know where I live."

"You bet, Louis."

"See ya!

"Well, Sean— What the hell is that?"

"I have a New York State trooper on my tail."

"How fast were you going?"

"I don't know . . . maybe a 100, maybe 105, or so."

"Maybe 105, or so? Are you out of your fucking mind?"

"Well, I wanted to blow out the engine."

"Pull over. And for God's sake, keep your hands on the steering wheel."

"Oh, don't get your panties in a wad. He can see we're cops." Having done two tours of duty in Iraq, O'Keeffe often told people that getting shot at quickly changes one's priorities.

"Just roll down your window and keep your hands on the wheel, Sean."

The state trooper, car roof lights flashing, pulled his dark blue sedan behind them and stopped. He sat in the car for a few minutes, obviously communicating with State Police Headquarters via a high-speed digital radio link regarding the make and model as well as the license number of the NYPD *Crown Vic* in front of him. When he was finished, he got out of his car, holstered his night stick, put on his wide-brimmed hat, and walked to where O'Keeffe and Martelli sat. They could see he carried the rank of sergeant. His name tag read 'Logan.'

"Good morning, gentlemen. Drivers license and registration, please."

O'Keeffe handed the trooper his NYPD leather badge holder and identification, drivers license, and vehicle registration.

"Well, well, well. What do we have here? One of New York City's Finest?"

The officer examined the three items, nodding his head as he looked first at O'Keeffe's police identification, then at the detective's drivers license, and finally, at the vehicle's registration papers.

Then, as he started to take out his ticket book, he looked O'Keeffe straight in the eye, and pointing his pen to his right, said, "Detective, I have to tell you. I've been behind that clump of trees back there for the last two hours, just waiting for you."

O'Keeffe, nonplussed, didn't skip a beat. "Well, Sergeant, I got here as quickly as I could."

Holy shit, thought Martelli. *This guy will triple the fine and take us before a magistrate in some jerkwater town before he lets us go. Hanlon will throw a shit fit!*

For a moment the officer just stared at him, and then broke into a wide grin and laughed. "I needed that, O'Keeffe."

Martelli raised his eyes to the Heavens. *Thank you, Lord.*

"This has been one crappy day, Detective, I can tell you that. I'm thankful for anything that'll take my mind off the accident I had to clear before dawn this morning. It was horrible . . . three cars, nine people, including four children. I knew one of the families . . . they were good God-fearing people. I couldn't do anything for any of 'em. From the look of things, they died instantly. Made me wonder if this wasn't the time to hang up my gun and badge and start my own home security firm."

He looked away for a few seconds, nodded as if he were saying to himself, *'Yes, maybe that's what I'll do,'* then turned his gaze back to O'Keeffe.

"So, what takes you guys so far out of your jurisdiction?"

Martelli leaned over and flashed his badge. "Martelli, here, Sarge. We're on our way to Lake George . . . murder investigation. Originally we thought the vic died of natural causes, but it turned out he was poisoned by someone who injected him with snake venom. He suffocated to death, though he may have suffered a heart attack at the same time. So now, we and the sheriff up there have a problem. Who, what, when, where, and why?"

"Well, at least you got the 'how' covered. It never stops, does it, guys?

"Okay, look, O'Keeffe, keep it under 80, would ya? I don't wanna have to scrape you off the pavement like I did those kids this morning."

"You got it, Sarge. And thanks."

■ *Theodore Jerome Cohen*

Eight

It was shortly after noon when O'Keeffe pulled his car into Dr. Allerton's parking lot on the west side of East Shore Drive. "I'll run in and get the file, Lou, if you want to get out and stretch a bit."

The men got out of the car. After performing a few shoulder, side, and triceps stretches, O'Keeffe bounded toward the building and through the front door of the doctor's office. Martelli also took the opportunity to do some upper-body stretches before reaching for his cell phone and speed dialing Deputy Coroner Antonetti.

"Hey, Louis . . . how's it going?"

"Well, we made it here in one piece. If we had gotten here any earlier, O'Keeffe would have set a new land-speed record."

Antonetti laughed. "So, how fast was he going this time?"

"As best I can tell, something on the order of 105 miles an hour. I don't know . . . I wasn't looking at the speedometer. If I had been, I probably would have been singing *Nearer My God To Thee.*"

"He's a pisser, that one."

"What about the Hayes exhumation? Anything happening?"

"He died intestate, with one relative . . . a nephew by the name of Kenneth Evans who lives and works in Princeton,

NJ. The estate is still under the control of an administrator, but I just received the court order to exhume the body. So, all that remains now is to make arrangements with the cemetery for the grave to be opened. I'm going to do that as soon as we hang up."

"Intestate, huh? Is it difficult to get a court order in such cases?"

"Believe it or not, Louis, this type of situation is far from unusual. More and more cases are popping up every day in the courts involving the exhumation of men who died intestate. Several recent cases, for example, involved posthumous paternity actions . . . specifically, the need for DNA testing to determine whether or not certain individuals are the children of the decedent."

"That gives a whole new meaning to the term 'lucky stiff,' Michael."

There was total silence on the line. Suddenly Antonetti burst into laughter. "I don't believe you said that, Louis."

Even Martelli had to laugh. "Yeah, it was pretty bad, all right. Who knows, the guy may have gotten 'lucky' just before he died. And now you're telling me we have cases involving treasure hunters claiming to be a decedent's nonmarital children clogging court dockets. That's a pretty sad commentary on society today."

"I agree."

"All right, Michael, keep me informed. We'll be heading to Weston's summer home in a few minutes, so if you need me, give me a ring."

"Take care, Louis."

Martelli terminated the call and looked at his watch. It had been ten minutes since his partner had entered the doctor's office, and there still was no sign of him. *Oh well,* thought Martelli, *he's probably waiting to thank the doctor personally, and no doubt she's with a patient.*

Another five minutes went by before O'Keeffe finally appeared with a manila envelope in his hand.

"I guess you had to wait for her to finish with a patient, huh?"

"Oh, no. We got to talking and— Lou, you should see her, she's a knockout! Anyway, we have a date tonight. She said she'll arrange a babysitter for her 10-year-old daughter, and we'll be able to have dinner and do a little dancing at the local night club before she has to get home to prepare for work tomorrow."

"What am I, chopped liver? I thought we could discuss the evidence we collect this afternoon, saving us a little time tomorrow."

O'Keeffe had a sheepish look on his face. "Sorry, Lou . . . I just couldn't resist the opportunity. Anyway, we're here to toss Weston's summer home, not his permanent residence. I doubt we'll be uncovering *that* much material of interest. And if you and I spent the evening in a motel room together, people would talk. You know these small towns." He winked at Martelli. "She's picking me up at 6 PM, at our motel. Don't wait up for me, Dad!"

Martelli shook his head. "If you hadn't saved my life last year, I'd put a slug through your 'small head' right now because it's pretty clear you're not thinking with the 'big one' on your shoulders!"

■ *Theodore Jerome Cohen*

<u>Nine</u>

Before leaving the doctor's parking lot, Martelli called the Lake George's Sheriff Office. "Sheriff Ward's out in the field now, Detective. Stand by. I'll transfer your call to his cell phone."

It took but a few seconds for the sheriff to pick up the call. "I'm investigating a robbery at the Hearthstone Point Campground, Detective Martelli. To save time, I suggest we meet at Weston's summer home on Still Bay? It's just north of the campground."

"That's a great idea. And please call me Lou."

"Only if you call me Geoff."

The sheriff was waiting for them when they arrived. One of the sheriff's deputies, who had been guarding the home, was sitting in his patrol car, which was parked off to the side of the driveway. Yellow crime scene tape cordoned off the entire front porch, and a notice prohibiting entry had been posted on the front door. The rear entry area had been similarly treated.

"Hi, Sheriff, I'm Lou Martelli. This is my partner, Sean O'Keeffe. You've spoken earlier, I believe."

The men shook hands.

"My pleasure, gents. I can't tell you how much I appreciate your help on this case. We don't get many homicides in this neck of the woods, especially one involving the use of exotic poisons. Obviously someone went to extreme lengths to cover up Phil's murder."

O'Keeffe took out his notebook and scribbled a few notes. Then, he looked up at the sheriff. "Geoff, did Mr. Weston have any enemies that you know of . . . anyone he owed money to or had a dispute with?"

"None I know of, Sean. Phil pretty much kept to himself. He came to town infrequently, and then, only to shop for groceries and the occasional piece of hardware he might need for his place. He always rented a car for the summer because he didn't own one of his own. Told me more than once it was simply too expensive to garage one in the city, and if he had to go anywhere down there, the cabs and subway were all he needed."

O'Keeffe pressed on. "So, you had reason to speak with him occasionally when he was here."

"No more or less than I spoke with any of his neighbors. I'm the kind of guy who does his job just by riding around a lot. In the old days, and in town, I'd patrol on foot . . . they called it 'pounding a beat.' There's no better way to get a sense of what's happening around here than to drive up and down the streets, stop and talk with people you see and check up on the ones you don't, and in general, simply keep an eye on things. There wasn't anything unusual about Phil or his activities in and around Lake George, at least as far as I could see. Hell, ask his neighbors. They'll tell you."

Martelli nodded. "Well, we've already spoken with his doctor in town. She saw him every year when he first arrived. He was in great health for his age and apparently had no problems to speak of. Maybe there's something inside the house that will give us a lead as to why someone would want to kill him."

O'Keeffe went to the back of his car, opened the trunk, and took out two small forensic kits and four evidence boxes. He gave one kit and two boxes to Martelli, keeping a kit and two boxes for himself.

The three men ducked under the yellow tape and approached the front door. O'Keeffe stopped and donned a pair of latex gloves. Martelli pulled two pairs out of his suit coat pocket and gave a pair to the sheriff before donning his.

"I got the key from Weston's daughter, Geoff." With that, he opened the door and the three men entered the front room of the house. The air was damp and stagnant, not unexpected given that the home had been closed for more than a week and the daytime outside temperatures had been in the mid- to high-80s Fahrenheit. "I'll open a window, Lou," said O'Keeffe, as he went to the large window overlooking the front porch and lifted the lower sash.

The sheriff motioned to the rear of the building. "If you open a window out back, Sean, we'll get a nice cross-breeze in here. It'll make it much more comfortable."

O'Keeffe turned and walked to the back of the house. He opened a window in the kitchen that overlooked the backyard. Almost immediately, a breeze began clearing the house of stagnant air, and the inside temperature began dropping.

Martelli and O'Keeffe took off their suit coats and laid them over the couch.

"Sean, do you want to take the upstairs? The sheriff and I'll toss the downstairs."

"Will do, Lou." O'Keeffe turned and walked up the stairs to the second floor, taking his forensic kit and two evidence boxes with him.

Martelli turned to the sheriff. "What we'll do, Geoff, is go on the assumption that Weston knew his killer and that it's possible the murder took place in this house. As such, we'll gather fingerprints from all doorknobs and other places where people might have put their hands and record their locations on a sketch we'll make showing the layout of the building. Sean's already doing that upstairs. I also want any personal items such as calendars, checkbooks, and things of that nature showing interactions with individuals and organizations as a function of date and time. For example, we found Weston's calendars for 2006, '07, '08, '09, and '10, but none for 2011. I have to believe he not only had one, but also, that he brought it with him to Lake George."

"If that's the case, Lou, it would be on his desk in the den. We should find it when we move into that room."

"That's great!

"Okay . . . let's get started here with the bookshelf to the left of the fireplace."

The men moved methodically through the books and other documents on the bookshelf, starting at the top. Most of the items on the shelves were old, some dating to the 1940s and earlier. They probably had belonged to the previous owner, judging from the inscriptions the men found on the inside front page, suggesting that they came with the house. About midway down the bookshelf, however, were several newer books, and these, not to Martelli's surprise—though they did leave the sheriff scratching his head—were on the subject of vampires.

"Well I'll be go to hell. Lou, what was Phil doing reading these?"

"Damned if I know. We found similar books in his library in Manhattan."

In his library in Lake George, the men found Créménés' *Mythologie du Vampire*, Melton's *The Vampire Book: The Encyclopedia of the Undead*, and a worn, almost unreadable

1910 edition of John Cuthbert Lawson's *Modern Greek Folklore and Ancient Greek Religion.*

"Let's bag and tag these, Geoff. I'll also make them the first entries on the inventory you and I are developing. Sean's creating a similar inventory upstairs. We'll head back to your office later and use your copier to print a set of inventories for your files. Then, all three of us will initial and date every page of both sets of inventories so that we'll both have complete sets for our files."

"Much obliged, Lou. Then, if someone should have a question regarding a specific piece of evidence, we won't have any problem identifying the item."

"At the same time, Geoff, I'd like to turn everything we collect today over to you for safekeeping tonight in your Evidence Room. I can't risk keeping the evidence with us in the motel tonight, and we need to ensure there's an unbroken chain-of-custody. The loss or compromise of one or more items could jeopardize our case down the line."

"Good thinking! We'll log it into our system when we get back to the station. You and Sean can pick it up at any time."

The two went through the remainder of the front room looking for evidence, but they found nothing. Before moving to the den, Martelli dusted the doorknobs in the room as well as the doorknob on the outside of the front door for fingerprints. Where prints were found, he lifted them using transparent lifting tape, being careful to note on a sketch of the building where each print was found. He also took photographs of the sites where prints were found.

The men then moved into the den. There, they found the missing 2011 calendar as well as a laptop, some copies of e-mails, personal correspondence from Weston's daughter and others, and both brokerage and bank statements. All were bagged and tagged as evidence and logged into the inventory.

"Did you find a cell phone, Geoff?"

"No, can't say I did. Unless Sean finds one upstairs, I'd have to guess he didn't use one."

The room was dusted for prints, and those found were preserved using lifting tape.

Other than fingerprints, the bathroom and kitchen yielded nothing.

Finally, Martelli lifted the prints found on the doorknobs inside and outside the backdoor to the home, which was located in the kitchen.

A search of the backyard yielded nothing.

By the time the sheriff and Martelli returned to the house from the backyard, O'Keeffe had finished his forensic investigation of the upstairs rooms.

"Not much up there, guys," he bellowed as he came down the stairs with a box of evidence.

"Hey, Sean." It was Martelli. "Did you find a cell phone up there?"

"No. Did you find one down here?

"No. Guess he only used a landline here."

Martelli turned to the sheriff. "Geoff, who found the body?"

"Arnold Braun, his next door neighbor, He was the one who called us. He had gone over to borrow some tools. He knew Phil was home because his car was in the driveway. When Arnold didn't get an answer after ringing the doorbell and knocking on the door, he peered through the living room window. That's when he saw Phil lying face-down on the front room floor and rushed back to his house to call 911."

"So, you were the one who responded to the call?"

"Yep . . . and Deputy Johnston out there . . . the fella in the marked patrol car."

"Okay, then it's safe to assume we're going to find both of your fingerprints on the doorknobs. We'll need to get your prints as well as Johnston's so we can eliminate them as prints of interest."

"Not a problem. We can each give you a set back at the office. I'll get you a set of Braun's as well. He can be a bit difficult, but I'll handle it."

"I appreciate that, Geoff. Would it be possible for me to talk with Deputy Johnston now . . . in here?

"Sure. Stand by."

Sheriff Ward went to the front door, stuck his head out, put two fingers in his mouth, and whistled to catch the deputy's attention. Once he saw the deputy turn his head toward the house, the sheriff motioned him in. It took but a minute for Johnston to appear in the front room.

"Deputy Johnston, I'm Detective Lou Martelli, NYPD. Please call me Lou. My partner is Detective Sean O'Keeffe."

"Pleased to meet you. You can call me Carl."

"Carl, Geoff tells us that the two of you responded to Arnold Braun's 911 call, is that correct?"

"Yes, sir . . . we drove here in our own vehicles and arrived about the same time. The sheriff also had called for an ambulance and a fire truck, which is SOP for the department. They arrived three minutes after we pulled into the driveway. Once we were able to break the door lock and get inside, the medic examined Mr. Weston. She said that as best she could tell, the man had been dead for at least a day. This was later confirmed by our coroner."

Martelli nodded. "So, when you arrived, the door was locked and there were no signs of forced entry, either at the front or back doors. Right?"

"Well, that's true for the front door," said the sheriff. "We didn't check the back door . . . had no reason to do that, given what we found. But as we saw, there's no damage back there. Whether or not the prints we lifted today will tell us anything is another story."

"Okay, I understand. By chance, did anyone take photographs of this room when you found Mr. Weston?"

The sheriff looked a little embarrassed. "Unfortunately, no. But again, Lou, it looked as if Phil had passed naturally. So, we didn't even think to take pictures. Who would have thought he was murdered?"

"Well, you're right about that, Geoff," said Martelli. "Frankly, if it were me, I'm not sure I would have taken pictures either. In truth, our lab had a hellava time determining the cause of death." *No sense in making the man feel badly*, thought Martelli, *he did the best he could under the circumstances.*

Martelli continued. "So, what we know is that he was found in this room, lying face-down, looking for all the world to see as a man who had died of a heart attack.

"Carl, would you do me a favor?"

"Sure, Lou."

"Please lie down on the floor in the same place and same position you saw Mr. Weston when you entered the room?"

The deputy walked to the bookshelf, got down on one knee, put his hands on the floor, and let himself down until he was lying prone . . . with his right hand extended, touching the books on the bottom shelf.

Martelli snapped photographs from several angles before resuming the conversation.

"It appears," noted Martelli, "he was in the process of reaching for something on the bookshelf when he was attacked."

"Wait a minute, Lou," the sheriff interrupted. "Why did it have to happen here? Couldn't the murderer have injected him earlier, say, upstairs or even outside at another location, with the venom taking effect much later?"

"Not possible. Look, and this is extremely sensitive so it can't be discussed except among ourselves, Weston was killed by someone who injected him with a lethal dose of Philippine Cobra venom. According to our deputy coroner, Michael Antonetti, it usually causes death by respiratory failure in as little as 30 minutes, perhaps less, depending on the amount of venom injected and the victim's age and physical condition. And if the perp holds his victim down until the poison takes effect, there is no way the person can call for help or seek medical attention.

"By the way, Antonetti didn't rule out the possibility that Weston could have suffered a heart attack as well, so it's easy to see how your medic and coroner were misled."

The sheriff nodded. "I see what you're saying, Lou."

Martelli took out his cell phone. "Hang on a minute, guys . . . I need to make a phone call." He speed dialed Antonetti, who picked up the phone immediately upon seeing who was calling.

"Louis, how goes the war?"

"So-so, Michael. I have a question."

"Shoot."

"When you were examining Weston, were you able to determine how the poison entered his system? Put another way, I would assume there were only two ways he could have received a lethal dose of venom . . . either a Philippine Cobra actually was made to bite him, or the venom was injected using a syringe and hypodermic needle."

"I checked his body. The bite of a Philippine Cobra doesn't cause significant tissue damage, so it's difficult to see. That said, I didn't see the telltale signs of a snake bite."

"Okay, no signs of a snake bite. What about a needle mark?"

"There was one, just below and to the back of his right ear lobe."

"Bingo! So, Weston probably knew, maybe even trusted, the person who killed him."

"Haven't you always told me, Louis? Be careful of the people closest to you. They're the ones who can do the most damage."

"I guess it's too late for Weston to learn that lesson."

"No kidding."

"Thanks, Michael, you've been a great help."

"My pleasure, Louis. Take care."

Martelli terminated the call and again turned his attention to the sheriff and his deputy.

"Did either of you happen to notice if there were signs of a struggle in this room?"

"I didn't see any, did you, Carl?"

"No, Sheriff."

Martelli turned to O'Keeffe. "Any signs of a struggle upstairs, Sean?"

"None I could see. The bed wasn't made, but that's not unusual for a bachelor's pad."

Martelli laughed. "I guess you'd know."

The sheriff looked around the room. "So, you're thinking that he let someone into the house . . . someone he knew . . . who perhaps overpowered him or, more likely, caught him completely off-guard in this room, injected him with snake venom, held him down until he was incapacitated, and then, left him to die."

Martelli nodded. "I don't see it happening any other way, Geoff. It had to be someone he knew well enough to let into the house."

The sheriff nodded. "I wonder if either of his neighbors saw anything. Braun found the body, but we never questioned him because, like I said, it looked like Phil died of a heart attack. Nor did we talk to Mrs. Goodman. She lives in the cottage on the other side of Weston's house. We never talked with her, either.

"Tell you what . . . let's finish up here and then, we'll walk over and talk with both of 'em.

"By the way, I'll keep the yellow crime scene tapes around the front and back of the building and the seals on both doors. We may need to return. And who knows . . . it may deter someone who's thinking about breaking in."

"Frankly, I'm not sure we need someone here 24x7, Geoff. Just check the place out once a day, if you would."

"I'd do that anyway, Lou."

■ *Theodore Jerome Cohen*

Ten

Arnold Braun was in his early 80s. Frail, with a full head of white hair in need of both a cut and a brushing, he was stooped over, barely reaching the height of 5 feet. A German immigrant and retired owner of a Manhattan tailor shop, he had undergone cataract surgery in his 60s, which had made him farsighted. He wore thick 'Coke bottle glasses' when conversing, something he did infrequently, or when reading, something he did voraciously.

Braun, a recluse, lived in a small two-story cottage set back some 75 feet from the lake. Neither a 'busybody' nor a gossip, he had few friends despite the fact he had lived in the community more than 20 years. He rarely ventured out, and when he did, it was only to shop for food or conduct business at the bank in town.

The sheriff and Martelli went to talk with Braun. Deputy Johnston and O'Keeffe waited in the deputy's air-conditioned car with the evidence taken from Weston's home.

Sheriff Ward pushed the button next to the front door several times, but heard nothing. Resigned to the possibility the doorbell was not working, the sheriff took to tapping gently but persistently on the door's window pane. Finally, the curtain parted and Braun's face appeared. Seeing the sheriff, he immediately opened the door, but only wide enough to peer out at the men.

The odor emanating from the home was overwhelming, a mixture of musty books, moldy newspapers and magazines, and mildewed wood.

Martelli could see the front room was stacked floor to ceiling with books, magazines, and newspapers, with only a small pathway available to walk from the front door to the back of the house.

Great, thought Martelli . . . *another Collyer situation! I'm not so sure we want to go in!*

The Collyer brothers, Homer Lusk Collyer and Langley Wakeman Collyer, both of whom died in 1947, became famous for their compulsive hoarding. Their home at the corner of 128th Street and Fifth Avenue in Manhattan not only had been filled with everything imaginable that the two collected, but also, had been booby trapped by the brothers to protect against intruders. At the end, both were found dead surrounded by 140 tons of collected items.

"Arnold, this is Detective Louis Martelli of the New York Police Department. We're investigating Phil's death. Seems it might not have been from natural causes after all. Do you mind if we come in for a minute and have a chat?"

"Yes, I mind. Go avay. I don't vanna get involved."

Even after 64 years in the United States, Braun spoke with a heavy German accent.

"We understand, Arnold, but it would be very helpful if you could just answer a few questions. We'll stay out here. I promise, this will only take a few minutes."

Braun shrugged his shoulders, as if to say, 'okay, okay.'

"Mr. Braun, did you see or speak with Mr. Weston often?"

"Ve used to talk some in da summer, vhen he was at da lake. He vas a nice man, vonce upon a time. Lofed books.

Sometimes he vud let me read tings from his library, but he vas always vanting dem back right avay . . . alvays vith the 'Vhen are you going to return my books?' or 'Vhen are you going to finish reading dat book I lent you?'

"Books vere meant to be savored, Detective. Dey cannot be devoured like a dog chewing on a piece of meat. So, I borrowed less and less from him as time vent on. Truthfully speaking, he vas becoming a pain in da ass.

"And den, a few years ago, he gets on dis vampire kick. Dat's all he vould talk about vhen I vas over der. And dat's vhen da visits began."

The sheriff cocked his head. "What visits were those, Arnold?"

"It started five years ago. A young couple vit a little girl vould visit him vonce every summer. They vould only stay vone day, and den, only vor an hour or two. He said dey alzo ver interested in vampires."

"Mr. Braun, do you remember anything about the couple? How they looked, what they wore, the type of car they drove, anything at all?"

"Not really. In all, I saw dem only three times together, starting, maybe, in 2006. Cars I don't know. I still drive da same car I purchased in 1985, and even den, it vas used. Maybe dey vas Middle Eastern, I don't know."

Martelli continued. "So, has this couple and the child been here yet this summer?"

"No, not dis summer. Dey didn't come last summer needer." Braun put his right hand next to his head and started wagging his forefinger. "But the man vas here—alone—da day before Phil died. I saw him drive up—he vas in a different car dis time—and he only stayed vor 20 minutes. Den he left. I didn't even see Phil vave goodbye like he alvays used to. I thot dat vas strange."

The sheriff looked at Martelli. "Do you have everything you need, Lou?"

"I think so, Geoff.

"Mr. Braun, you've been most helpful. Would you please be so kind and call Sheriff Ward if anything else comes to mind that you think might be helpful? What you've told us today is most interesting, and will, I think, help us with our investigation."

Braun nodded and flapped his left hand at them, as if to brush them away. "Zei gezunt." Then he slammed the door in their faces.

Eleven

'W'ell, that went well," said Martelli as he and Sheriff Ward walked across the grass in the front of Weston's home on their way to Diane Goodman's cottage.

The sheriff laughed. "Thank God we caught him on a good day, Lou."

"Yeah, well, lots of luck getting his fingerprints. I suspect you'll have to hogtie the gentleman and haul him into town before that's done."

"Aw, he'll settle down. I'll bring some schnapps with me tomorrow, and we'll finish up before he has no more than two shots."

Deputy Johnson and O'Keeffe, sitting in the deputy's patrol car, appeared to be engaged in an animated conversation involving the shooting of rifles at targets located well above their heads. "My guess is war stories," the sheriff said, laconically. "Johnson was in the 10th Mountain Division . . . Nuristan Province, Iraq, I believe."

Martelli chuckled. "O'Keeffe was over there, as well. I'm sure they'll have more than enough stories to tell each other. Some may even be true."

The men continued walking to Mrs. Diane Goodman's cottage, a traditional two-story lake home that sat 100 feet back from the water. They had barely finished climbing the front steps when the door opened."

"Well, if it isn't Sheriff Ward. How are you, Geoff?"

"Just fine, Diane. Thanks for asking. This here is Detective Louis Martelli of the New York Police Department. We were wondered if you might have a little time to answer a few questions regarding Phil Weston."

She smiled broadly. "Of course, of course. Please come in. It's so nice to have company."

Goodman, a widow, was in her mid-70s. Short, with gray hair, she was more than a few pounds overweight. 'I'm big boned,' is what she told her closest friends when they would discuss their weight problems while playing Mahjongg on Wednesday afternoons. Goodman was dressed in a bright rainbow-striped housecoat and smelled as if she had just taken a scented bath.

She stepped back, motioning them to step into the screened porch that encircled the lower level of the house on three sides. On the left, in the far corner of the porch, the men could see a dining area. A couch was positioned to the right of the dining table, the first of several pieces of furniture that Goodman and her guests used when they read or simply relaxed while enjoying a refreshing lake breeze.

During the winter, storm windows replaced the screens that had been hung over the windows for the summer. As well, the dark green canvas awnings on the lake side of the house had been rolled up to let the sun and lake breezes in. The awnings would be dropped in early November to protect the house from winter's onslaught.

To the right of the porch's front door was a door that led to the cottage's kitchen while in front of them, another door led to the living room.

"Gentlemen . . . please . . . go into the living room. I'll join you in a minute. How do you take your coffee?"

"I'll take mine with milk, Diane."

"Fine, Geoff. And you, Detective?"

"Please call me Lou, Diane. I take mine black . . . straight up."

"Okay, Lou. I'll be back in a minute. Please, make yourselves at home."

Martelli looked around. The living room was an anachronism. The year may have been 2011 but the room was painted and decorated as if it were as early as the mid-1930s but certainly not much later than the outbreak of World War II. The walls and ceiling were painted light beige while large, thick, Persian carpets covered the hardwood floor. A darkly stained upright piano stood next to the stairs leading to the second floor, which housed three small bedrooms and a bathroom. Opulent chairs, carefully positioned around a coffee table in the center of the living room, were covered in vintage brocade fabrics while several display cabinets filled with family pictures and porcelain artifacts lined two windowless walls. Appropriately placed end tables covered with knick-knacks and tchotchkes rounded out the room's furnishings.

Wow, thought Martelli, *for all intents and purposes, time has stood still. This room hasn't changed in 75 years.*

"Here you are, gentleman. Geoff, I'll let you pour your own milk. And I brought something for us to nosh on while we talk. Just don't tell Dr. Allerton I ate any of these."

She set a plate of homemade cinnamon rolls on the coffee table. "She's been warning me about my blood sugar level, so I'm trying to cut back on my sweets. But I still cheat a little, now and then." She put the forefinger of her right hand over her lips.

Martelli picked right up on what she was saying. "Your secret is safe with me, Diane."

She giggled.

"This really is a beautiful home you have," he continued, attempting to break the ice.

"It was given to my father by his uncle in the early 1950s. They worked together during World War II. When the uncle retired to Florida, he gave my father this home in exchange for one dollar. We used it as a summer home until my father died in 1967, and then, my mother and I lived in it until she died in 2005. Now I have it. It's just like it always was. Nothing's changed."

Martelli smiled. "I imagine that's a great comfort to you."

"Not everything has to change, Lou. It's possible to find happiness even in the simplest of things . . . a cool lake breeze, fireflies on a hot summer night, a spring thunderstorm. They are as enjoyable and comforting to me now as they were in 1953."

She smiled, closed her eyes momentarily, and nodded. Then she turned and stared out through the room's large picture window, across the porch toward the gazebo in the back yard, and beyond to the lake, as if in her mind's eye she still could see her family as they were when she was a little girl. Slowly she turned back to look at the men.

"Well, Detective, you didn't come all this way to hear me talk about this house and my family. How can I help you?"

"Diane, I can't go into too much detail because of the nature of my investigation, but I will tell you that Mr. Weston did not die of natural causes."

Goodman stopped chewing her food and stared at Martelli. "What?"

"I know this will come as a shock. We don't know who killed him. Nor do we have a motive."

Goodman swallowed and then sat silently, attempting to make sense of something that clearly made no sense to her. Slowly, she wiped her mouth with a linen napkin.

"I can't believe it."

The men let what Martelli had just told her sink in.

Finally, the sheriff spoke. "Diane, if there's anything you can remember about Phil regarding the last few days before his death, it could be of immense importance to our investigation."

"Well, let me think. Phil and I never spoke, of course. Never had any reason to. Years ago he made it crystal clear that he wasn't interested in establishing any kind of neighborly relationship with me. Every once in a while I'd see him talking to Arnold Braun—he's another strange one, that Braun fellow—but even those exchanges appeared to have petered out a while back."

Sheriff Ward picked up the conversation. "Did Phil have any visitors over the years that you recall, Diane?"

"Let's see. Oh, yes, several years ago there was a couple and their daughter who came to visit him in the summer. If I remember correctly, they were here two or three times . . . always in the middle of July. But they didn't show up last year. Nor did I see the family this year."

"Are you sure about that, Diane?"

"Oh, yes. Other than that couple and their child, no one ever came to see Phil. Their visits aren't something I would forget."

"Do you remember anything about them? For example, what did they look like? What kind of car did they drive? Anything at all?"

"Well, they weren't Caucasians, if that's what you mean."

"'How so?" asked Martelli.

71

"Their skin seemed darker. And their features were different. They could have been Middle Eastern."

"And their car? Do you know the make?"

"What do I know? My father always drove a Packard *Clipper* . . . the last one was turquoise and white with big whitewall tires. Now, *that* was a real car, not like the junk they sell today."

Martelli laughed. "I take that as a 'no.'"

Goodman laughed. "Your mother didn't raise no dumb kid, Lou. But I can tell you this. The man showed up over there—alone—the day before Phil was found dead, and he wasn't driving the same car he drove when his family—at least I think it was his family—came to Phil's on earlier visits. The car he drove this time was small and gray; when he came with his family, he drove a larger car . . . one of those, what do they call them? Oh, yes . . . SUVs. And that one was white."

Martelli was busy taking notes as Sheriff Ward asked the next question. "How long did he stay this time?"

"Oh, maybe 20 minutes, 25 minutes, tops. Which surprised me, because before, when the three of them came to visit, they always stayed a couple of hours. Anyway, I was puttering around the porch when I saw him pull Phil's front door shut. Then, he turned and walked to his car—"

"Did he appear to be in a hurry?"

"Not particularly. He threw his briefcase in the back seat, got in the driver's seat, started the engine, and drove away. I didn't think anything of it."

Martelli thought for a minute. "If I brought an artist up here, Diane, is it possible the two of you might be able to come up with a sketch of the man?"

"I doubt it, Lou. Not that I wouldn't be willing to give it a try, but I only saw the side of the man's head, and from quite a distance at that."

"Okay, I understand. Just one or two more questions, then. Could you venture a guess as to the age of the people in the family? We understand there also was a child . . . a girl."

"Well, when I last saw the woman, which was two years ago, I'd say she was in her early 30s. The little girl could not have been more than 4 years old at the time. I don't know . . . she looked very young and frail."

"And the man?"

"I'd say he was in his mid- to late 30s."

The men finished their cinnamon rolls and coffee, wiped their mouths, and stood up.

Goodman looked up at them. "Anything else I can do for you, gentlemen?"

"Well," said Martelli, "I sure could use a bathroom."

"I'll second that," said the sheriff."

"It's at the top of the stairs, on your right. But don't flush the toilet until you've both used it! I'm on a well here. If you both flush, you'll stir up the sand at the bottom of the well, and then, I'll have problems with my pump!"

■ *Theodore Jerome Cohen*

Twelve

The trip back to the sheriff's office was uneventful. Once there, Martelli and O'Keeffe helped the sheriff make copies of the inventories they had created for the evidence gathered. Then, the three men initialed and dated every sheet on the original documents and the copies. That done, Martelli put the original document in his briefcase. The evidence was locked in the sheriff's Evidence Room, and Martelli and O'Keeffe left for the night.

Sean was in high spirits. "Well, I'd say we had a rather successful day, Lou."

"I agree. Given who we were working with, I think we got about as much information from Weston's neighbors as was possible. As for the evidence, we'll have to wait until we get back to the city before we'll know what we have. At the least, we now have the missing 2011 calendar. I was tempted to sign it out so that I could go through it tonight, but I didn't want to take a chance that something might happen to it."

"I think you did the right thing."

"So, what's the plan?"

"Well, I want to check in and take a shower. Susan is picking me up for dinner at 6, and then, we'll go dancing for a while. She has to work tomorrow, so it won't be a late night. What are you going to do?"

"I think I'll check in, give Steph a call, and then, go out for a bite at that restaurant we passed on our way into town. After that, I'm just going to relax."

"A little R&R never hurts, my friend."

Thirteen

Martelli threw his suitcase on the bed, headed for the bathroom, and splashed cold water on his face. After drying it with a face towel, he sat down on the bed and speed dialed his house. It took only two rings before he heard his wife's voice.

"Ah, the Italian Stallion, galloping through the New York countryside, igniting lust in the hearts of young maidens and envy in the minds of their boyfriends."

"I'm not so sure about that galloping part . . . maybe a little cantering, perhaps, and a trot now and then."

She laughed. Their relationship was as fresh and youthful as the day they met.

"Well, you still seem able to get out on the dance floor at the precinct's Christmas Party and put the younger officers to shame."

"Speaking of dancing, you'll never guess who has a dinner date tonight, followed by a night of dancing at a local night club."

"Sean? You're kidding!"

"Just like you women. You can't stand to see a handsome, single, happy-go-lucky guy enjoying life to the fullest. As far as you're concerned, a man isn't fulfilled unless he's married and tied down with ten children."

"Keep it up, Detective-Investigator Louis Martelli, Master of All He Surveys, and your sex life going forward will give new meaning to the word 'celibate!'"

"Ha! We'll see who caves first!"

They laughed as if they were teasing each other before classes began during their high school years.

"So, what are the kids doing?"

"Jeff is helping Tiffany prepare for a debate she'll participate in tomorrow, and—"

"Debate? What's the question?"

"Should there be a path to citizenship for illegal immigrants who have been here for at least ten years and have made contributions to US society?"

"Wow, our school district isn't afraid to tackle the hard problems, is it?"

"No, and I'm thankful for that. It's a different world today than the one we grew up in, Lou. These are the kinds of classroom exercises that will help our children think for themselves when they're on their own."

"And Rob . . . what's he doing?"

"He's studying for a science test . . . something having to do with radio. If you think I understand the subject, guess again. Each student had to build a crystal set receiver as part of this unit of study, and now, they're going to be tested on how it works. He loves it. He has a friend studying with him."

"And you?"

"Don't ask!"

"That doesn't sound good."

"My day was hell, Lou. I had to fire two independent contractors."

"What?"

"One of our jobs, a huge multi-million-dollar effort, came in more than $20,000 over budget. I had the costs on that contract tuned to a fair-thee-well just a month ago because I getting ready to close it. So, I did another audit and found these two contractors had billed hours to a charge number for which they had not received authorization. The details were buried in some highly complex spreadsheets, believe me. But I performed some keyword searches and in no time, found the falsified charges. That's all I needed, and unfortunately, I had to fire them. Couldn't trust 'em anymore, Lou."

Martelli didn't say anything.

"Lou . . . did you hear what I said?"

"You bet! I'm sorry, Sweetheart. But you just gave me an idea for some work I want Dugan and O'Keeffe to do for me."

"Well, I'm happy *something* good came of my day!"

■ *Theodore Jerome Cohen*

Fourteen

'Well, if it isn't NYPD's World Champion Ballroom Dancer, the one, the only, Detective Sean O'Keeffe!"

O'Keeffe, dripping wet with a bath towel wrapped around his waist and a hairbrush in his right hand, had just opened the door to his motel room to let Martelli in. He had a big smile on his face.

"Lou, we had the most fantastic time. And what a terrific dancer she is! If it wasn't for the fact that she had to get up at 5:30 this morning, get her daughter off to school, and then do her rounds at the hospital, we would have danced until they closed."

Lou smiled. "I'm really happy for you, Sean. She seemed like a nice lady when I talked with her on the phone."

Sean walked back into the bathroom to finish drying off, comb his hair, and finish his morning ritual.

"Oh, she is. But life's dealt her some hard knocks, Lou. It hasn't been easy for her, believe me."

"In what way?"

"She lost her parents when she was 12 years old. They were killed in a boating accident. Her aunt on her father's side raised her. She was a professor at Albert Einstein

81

College of Medicine in Manhattan. It's from her aunt that she gets her passion for medicine.

"After pre-med at the University of Wisconsin-Madison, she interned at Harvard followed by a residency at the University of Virginia. That's where she met her husband, who also was from upstate New York. They were married almost immediately, and their daughter, Heather, was born a year later. After they finished their residencies in Charlottesville, they returned to upstate New York and opened a practice together in Lake George."

"What happened to her husband?"

"He died three years ago. It was tragic. Turns out he volunteered two weeks of his time each year to provide free medical care to the indigenous peoples of Alaska. His plane went down near Chalkyitsik while on a mission to save a dying child. Both he and the pilot were killed."

"That must have been pretty rough on her."

Sean came out of the bathroom in his briefs and proceeded to dress.

"It was. But she had her daughter and the practice she and her husband had started, so she vowed to carry on. She's one tough woman, Lou. Reminds me a lot of Steph. Tough as nails on the outside, but sweet and loving on the inside. You know what I mean?"

"Oh, yes."

"You'll both get to meet her at the Christmas party this year. I'm going to drive up, and bring her and her daughter down—"

"Steph will be thrilled, Sean. Susan's daughter can stay with us. As for you and the doctor, you're on your own."

"Thanks, Lou. I knew I could count on you."

"Just keep your speed below 75 when you drive up here and back, will you? The last thing you need is another

82

encounter with Sergeant Logan. He won't be so forgiving next time."

"I hear ya!"

■ *Theodore Jerome Cohen*

Fifteen

The men checked out of their motel rooms, grabbed a quick breakfast at the adjoining diner, and after picking up the evidence they had taken from Weston's home from the Lake George Sheriff's Office, set out on their return trip to New York City.

Martelli spent the early part of the trip apprising O'Keeffe of his and Sheriff Ward's discussions with Arnold Braun and Diane Goodman. "Our perp, it appears, is of Middle Eastern descent, Sean. Until two years ago, he visited Weston during the summer a few times with a woman that may have been his wife. They also had a young girl with them. Those visits lasted about two hours each. Apparently, they didn't show up in 2009 or this year, but the man was seen at Weston's on the day before his body was discovered. For both Braun's and Goodman's accounts, he only was in the house for 20 minutes . . . perhaps slightly longer. That would fit the timeline . . . inject Weston with the venom, hold him down, and then, once he was sure the man went into respiratory failure, leave."

"Do you think either neighbor, working with a sketch artist, might be able to help us come up with a composite drawing of the perp?"

"I don't think so. Goodman would have been our best witness for that option. But she said she only saw the perp from the side, and even then, it was from quite a distance. You know yourself that there's a pretty good distance between her home and the front steps of Weston's house.

"And I don't have a clue as to what's going on with Braun's eyes. The lenses he was wearing when he answered the door looked to be one-quarter inch thick. Maybe he's farsighted . . . I don't know . . . but man, how he can see *anything* is beyond me."

"You're probably right, Lou. It doesn't sound like we're going to get a reasonable likeness from either of them. So what's your plan?"

"I'm hoping that we'll find something in the calendar we pulled from Weston's place yesterday as well as those we found in his Manhattan apartment. Maybe Weston marked his calendar in some way with a name or phone number on the day he was expecting the couple and their child to visit. That would give us the lead we need to work backwards and at the least, I'm hoping, learn the identity of the man. Right now, he's the only person of interest we—"

Martelli's cell phone rang. It was Antonetti.

"Yes, Michael."

"Lou, I just got a call from Sergeant Reynolds at CSU."

"Terrific! What did he have to say?"

"Weston never had blood drawn by any certified pheresis center within 50 miles of New York City. The only things Reynolds turned up were records of blood samples taken for tests prescribed by his doctor in Manhattan."

"I didn't think his anemia was the result of blood donations, Michael, but we had to run the traps."

"Yeah, I know. Reynolds also told me to tell you that they went back to Weston's apartment and went through it again for fingerprints and other forensic evidence. They're processing it now."

"That's great. Please give him a call and thank him, would you?"

"Not a problem."

"And how are you doing on the Hayes exhumation?"

"We're bringing the body out of the ground at 9 this morning. I should have it in my table by the time you get back to the city. Stop down . . . I may have something to tell by then."

"I'll be there as soon as we take the stuff we're carrying to the Evidence Room. I don't want anything to break the chain of custody. My gut tells me this is going to turn out to be one of the more important cases we've worked on in the last several years."

"I'll be here. Just come down when you're ready."

"See ya later, Michael."

Martelli terminated the call and speed dialed Alexa Lindsay Beauvais, the Department's senior forensic financial analyst. Her phone rang four times before it automatically switched to her cell phone. Two more rings and Beauvais answered.

"Hey, Lou."

"Hi, Alexa, how are you?"

"I'm okay . . . just spending a little time with my mother. She's always better in the morning, so I try to spend an hour with her at least twice a week before heading to the office."

"How's she doing since you moved her to the Alzheimer's home in Manhattan?"

"Not well, but thanks for asking. The good news is that I no longer fear she'll set my apartment on fire by forgetting something she put in the oven. You remember what happened last year."

"Man, do I ever. If the super hadn't smelled something burning, you could have had a real problem."

"You bet. I think I moved her at just the right time, and I have no regrets—"

"Nor should you, Alexa . . . you've been a saint."

"Thanks, Lou, but it's been . . . difficult."

Lou could hear her choke up. He waited until she composed herself.

"But the bad news is—" She burst into tears. "Oh, Lou, she doesn't know who I am anymore."

Martelli heard Beauvais sobbing. He said nothing, allowing her time to work through the moment.

"Some friends say to me, 'Why do you go to visit her so often even though she doesn't know you?' I know they mean well, but they don't understand. *I* know *her*. She is my mother. She took care of me all those years when I was growing up, and now, it's my turn to take care of her."

"Maybe I could go with you to visit her someday."

"Oh, would you do that, Lou? She would love it. She loves talking with men . . . she always said they are so interesting. She and my dad used to have the most stimulating conversations that ranged over a wide variety of topics . . . politics, religion, music, art . . . you name it, they discussed it. And at parties, there wasn't a subject on which she didn't hold an informed opinion.

"It's been so sad to see how this disease robbed her of her intellect. So, yes . . . it would be wonderful to have you with me some day, if only to have a third person to share the conversation."

"Consider it done. We'll just make time, perhaps some Saturday or Sunday, when things quiet down a little."

"Now you're the saint, Louis Martelli."

"I suspect the Good Lord might have a slightly different opinion when it comes to that."

She laughed. "Well, you didn't call to hear my problems. How can I help you?"

"Look, I don't want to take you away from your mother. If you have some time tomorrow morning, say around 10 AM or so, can you drop by my office at the First Precinct for a chat? I have a case that I think you will find intriguing, and I need your analytical skills to help solve it."

"I'll be there."

"Thanks, Alexa. I knew I could count on you."

■ *Theodore Jerome Cohen*

<u>Sixteen</u>

'M'ichael, I'm sorry . . . I got here as quickly as I could. It took much longer than I expected to log the things from Weston's cottage into evidence."

It was mid-afternoon. Martelli had just entered the morgue after running out to grab a hotdog, bag of chips, and soft drink from a street vendor parked in front of 1PP.

"You don't mind if I finish eating while you talk, do you, Michael?"

"Not at all, my boy."

"So, tell me, what's the story on Hayes? Have you had a chance to look over his corpse?"

"Yes, Louis, and you're not going to believe what I found."

"Well?"

"There were traces of garlic in his oral cavity." He paused for effect. "And look here—"

Antonetti pointed to Hayes's corpse, which lay on the table in front of them.

"See that hole in his chest. Here's the stake I pulled from it."

He held up a small, meticulously carved wooden stake that had been embedded in the corpse's chest, just above where the man's heart had been before it had been removed during the embalming process.

"What?"

"You heard me. And I think we can be pretty sure the person who embalmed the body didn't implant the small piece of wood I found."

"Unbelievable!"

Martelli shook his head. "Damn. It's too late to get the videotapes from the church where Hayes's funeral service was held. I'm sure they've been recycled. No matter. We have a problem. Not only are we dealing with a serial killer, but a serial killer who believes, for whatever reason, that his victims are vampires. The question is, how many more bodies are buried out there of people who were killed and desecrated in the same ways Weston's and Hayes's corpses were . . . and for the same reason?"

"Perhaps more importantly, Louis, how many more victims are yet to die at the hands of this vampire slayer?

"God help you if the press gets wind of this."

"Damn."

He threw the remains of his lunch in the wastebasket and headed for the door. "I better brief Hanlon. Now!"

Seventeen

'H ave you lost your fucking mind?" Captain Hanlon of the First Precinct almost spit out his coffee when Martelli told him his theory of what had happened to Weston's and Hayes's corpses.

"Vampires? Damn, Martelli, you've come up with some, shall we say, 'interesting' theories over the years—like that time last year when you thought the FBI was bugging your telephones—but this takes the cake. Shut the damn door before someone calls Bellevue and has us both hauled away."

Martelli leaned back in his chair, and reaching out with his left hand, sent the office door slamming into its frame.

"Yes, sir, I know it sounds strange—"

"Strange? *Strange?* It sounds like something right out of those vampire movies the teenagers are so crazy about these days.

"Let me get this straight. You expect me to believe that someone not only is going around killing people, but also, is going to great lengths to make sure their victims never rise from the dead?"

"That's it in a nutshell, Captain. Ask Antonetti. He'll tell you."

Hanlon shook his head.

"Consider this, Captain. We have two bodies in the morgue, one of which was just exhumed this morning, from

93

which our coroners have pulled slugs fired from the same gun.

"In one case dating back a year, the slug was fired into the vic's heart during what we *thought* was a botched robbery. After the body was exhumed, we found garlic in the corpse's mouth and a small wooden stake in the chest above where the heart would have been.

"In a second, more recent case, that of a man who had been poisoned at Lake George, the slug was fired *through* the casket wall into his chest, and garlic was found stuffed in his mouth. This took place just before the start of the deceased's funeral service, while the corpse was available for viewing in a church not far from here.

"So, unless someone simply enjoys celebrating the Festival of the Dead—Halloween to you and me—nonstop throughout the year, what we have here, Captain, is nothing less than a serial killer who is committed to ensuring his victims never walk the earth again."

Hanlon pounded the desk with his fist. "What we have, Martelli, is a *freaked-out whacko* who should be committed, that's what we have! And *you* need to stop him. Fast!

"Oh, and Martelli, I don't want *anyone* talking to the media about this. Can you imagine what would happen if this got out? It would become the most sensational story since . . . shit, I don't know . . . Madoff!

"Just find the son-of-a-bitch who's doing this. And the sooner, the better!"

"I'll do my best, Captain. Right now, I need to get back to 1PP and talk to Dugan, my IT specialist."

Eighteen

'Hey, Dugan, I have a job for you and O'Keeffe." It was Martelli, calling from the entrance to the IT Laboratory as he entered Missy's domain shortly after leaving Hanlon's office in the First Precinct.

"O'Keeffe? You mean Pretty Boy Floyd?" She let out one of her maniacal laughs that could be heard a mile away.

"Don't let Sean hear you call him that, or he'll put a 9mm slug right through the center of your forehead without batting an eye!"

"You know, I actually think he would do that. But I do so love him. Mark my word, he's going to end up chasing someone until they catch him."

"It may be sooner than you think. He was smitten by a doctor on our trip upstate. But let him tell you about her. From what he told me on the way back this morning, she sounds like a fine woman."

"Sean? Smitten? Miracles do happen. I can't wait to hear what he has to say. In all the time I've known him, I don't think I've learned five things about his personal life."

"I know. He's a closed book."

"So, what's on your mind?"

"These two cases I'm working on—"

"Two? I thought you were working only on the Weston case."

95

"No, we're reopening the Hayes case . . . in fact, to commemorate the event, we just reopened Hayes's grave." He started to laugh, having struck himself funny.

"Nice, Martelli . . . you know you're going to Hell for that." She started to laugh with him.

"I'm sorry . . . Antonetti pulled Hayes's corpse out of the ground this morning. He found garlic in the man's mouth and a stake embedded in his chest. And for God's sake, keep it to yourself, will ya? Hanlon blew a gasket when I briefed him 20 minutes ago. He's scared to death the media will get wind of what's happening, and he'll end up on the receiving end of a shitstorm. He knows we only have a limited amount of time before someone says something. It always happens. Some jerk in the Department will leak the story to the press for a few measly bucks and then, there'll be hell to pay. So we need to work fast."

"What do you want Sean and me to do?"

"First, go down to the Evidence Room and sign out all of the digital media from the Weston and Hayes evidence boxes. You'll find two computers for Weston. I'm not sure what you'll find in Hayes's box.

"Then, sift through the e-mails and documents on the harddrives and other storage devices you find. Use these keywords to guide your search. Print a copy of anything that pops up on your search."

Martelli handed her a sheet of paper containing a table of keywords.

Missy scanned the list. "This shouldn't be a problem. After we log any documents we print we make into evidence, Sean can bring them to the precinct and review them with you."

Vampires	Werewolves	Blood
Drink	Coffin	Fangs
Corpse	Spirit	Wax Cross
Grave	Garlic	Lemon
Pottery	Seeds	Millet
Sand	Rice	Mustard Seeds
Dracula	Virgin	Graveyard
Cemetery	Shadow	Mirror
Stake	Needle	Brick
Exorcism	Bullet	Dismemberment
Holy Water	Boiling Water	Drowning
Spirit	Demon	Devil

"That's exactly what I wanna to do. And if you can think of anything else—"

"How about the vic's cell phones? I think we should go through them, assuming they owned such devices. At the least, we'd have their contact lists, lists of any calls made or received that still can be retrieved, and the like."

"Good thinking. Weston, apparently, didn't own a cell phone . . . at least, we didn't find one. See what you can come up with through his landline provider. Hayes may have used a cell phone, though."

"I'll check it out."

"One more thing. Do a cross-check between the digital media belonging to both men for all possible surnames. I assume that somewhere, you have a directory of such names."

"Oh, yes . . . and it's humongous! I'll run English, Spanish, French, and Italian."

"Add Israeli, Iranian, Iraqi, and any other Middle Eastern surnames you can put your hands on."

"You're not telling me something, Lou."

"Weston had a visitor on the day before he was killed. Two witnesses described the man as appearing to be of Middle Eastern descent. Now, that doesn't rule out the possibility the person was born here and has a name more like those traditionally found in the States. But on the other hand, there's always the possibility that either he immigrated to the States or was born here to parents who named him according to the traditions of their native country. The same may be true of his wife and child."

"I understand. What about the documents already in hardcopy format?"

"I'm meeting with Beauvais tomorrow about those. I'll ask her to watch for the same things you're looking for when she goes through bank statements, cancelled checks, e-mails, and other miscellaneous documents. It'll be more difficult for her to do this because she won't be able to automate the process to any great extent. So I'm counting on her memory to recall having seen something as she sifts through the material."

"I'll get started now. When do you think Sean will be here to help sort things out?"

"He's completing some paperwork for us on another case we recently closed. The ADA's waiting for his sworn statement. I don't think he'll be able to start until tomorrow morning. Better begin without him, and he'll join the party as soon as he's free."

Nineteen

'So, do you always cheat at solitaire?" It was Alexa Lindsay Beauvais, arriving for their 10 AM meeting. Beauvais was a slender woman in her mid-30's. Standing 5 feet, 8 inches tall, she had shiny black hair that fell well below her shoulders. Her coal-black eyes could drill right through a person. Now, she was boring a hole directly into Martelli's eyes over the tops of her fashionable glasses, which were perched slightly down the slope of her bobbed nose.

Lou, who was taking a short break from filling out Department paperwork, looked up.

"I didn't cheat!"

"Yes, you did. I saw you draw that last card from the bottom of the deck!"

Martelli smiled. "You know me too well."

"Apparently that Las Vegas casino where you were playing blackjack during your children's spring break earlier this year knows you pretty well, too."

"Who told you about that?"

"A little birdie."

"Scheesch . . . Sean can't keep his mouth shut for one minute!"

"Sean? Give me a break. He's as tightlipped as a priest who's just heard your confession. Actually, it was Stephanie. She called the other day to ask about my mother."

"So, they caught you card counting, huh?"

"Oh, it wasn't anything special. I was just using a simple High-Low system. It probably gave me a one percent advantage over the house in a game with six decks."

"How much did you win?"

"A little more than $10,000 before the floor manager started to watch the table too closely."

"What did you do with the money?"

"Well, after paying for the trip and sending a $2,000 donation to the Police Unity Tour, I gave the rest to Steph. You know what they say . . . 'Happy wife, happy life.'"

She laughed. "Lou, are there any more like you?"

"I'm sure there's a great guy out there for you, Alexa. You just haven't found each other yet."

She nodded. "I guess.

"Anyway, you asked me to drop by."

"Yes, yes . . . pull up a chair, and I'll brief you on the cases Sean and I are working. I'm not sure you'll even believe what I'm about to say."

Martelli apprised her on how Weston and Hayes had been murdered, and on the need for absolute silence in all matters pertaining to their cases.

"These are strange things, all right, Lou. But I've heard of stranger things happening.

"Do you remember that case—I think it was in 2006— when a vampiress was accused of savagely sinking her teeth into a girl's neck in what the *New York Post* described as a series of bizarre bloodlettings involving three high school girls in Jamaica, New York?"

"Yeah, I remember that. A girl by the name of Melendez said she was waiting for her school bus when a 15-year-old 'vampire' started slashing her face and then, sank her teeth into the victim's neck. According to Melendez, the girl was going for her jugular vein. The attack left blood flowing all over her face and neck. The attacker even had Melendez's skin in her mouth."

"That's right, Lou. Some people were saying that it reminded them of Elizabeth Kosovo's book *The Historian*.

"And then there was a case in the German courts in 2002 involving a man named Daniel Ruda, who put an ad in a lonely hearts column."

"And you remember this *how*?"

"Well, I have a very good memory. Besides, I had a lot of time to sit and read while I was keeping my mother company.

"But that aside, I was so startled by it that it just stuck in my head. You know what happens to your memory when the adrenalin starts flowing."

"How did the ad read?"

"'Vampire seeks princess of darkness that hates everyone and everything.'"

"Did anyone answer?"

"Oh yes, a woman who eventually became his wife. Her name was Manuela. They were married on the 6th day of the 6th month in 2001 and made a pact to kill on the 6th of July. That's how they derived the number '666,' the biblical sign of the Devil.

"In any event, they invited a friend of Daniel Ruda's, one Mr. Hackert by name, to a party. After Ruda hit Hackert with a hammer, Manuela told Ruda to stab Hackert in the heart. After killing him, they both drank the victim's blood and prayed to Satan.

"Oh, and you'll find this interesting, Lou."

"What's that?"

"When she was 16, Manuela ran away to England, where she met other Satanists and engaged in 'bite parties.'"

"Bite parties. Sounds like fun. Didn't one of your boyfriends ever give you a hicky?"

"Well, it was a little more than that. Those attending drank each other's blood. Ruda is said to have told the court that he, personally, had a 'lust for blood' . . . that he liked the metallic salty taste."

"Well, we didn't find any bite marks on Weston's body, but there certainly is anecdotal evidence that someone took blood from his body over the years. His doctors observed bruises on his body when they examined him, and blood tests showed him to be anemic."

"From what you've told me, Lou, I would say we're dealing with a cult, and Weston and Hayes were but two of its members. It's also possible that the couple who visited Weston in Lake George was part of that cult, given that the man was seen at Weston's home one day before his body was discovered. Moreover, there may be other cult members in this area, as well."

"I agree. Unfortunately, that means we may have more victims buried out there."

"Or murders yet to be committed."

"That's a comforting thought," Martelli remarked, facetiously.

"So, how can I help you?"

"When you have time this morning, please go down to the Evidence Room and pull all of Weston's and Hayes's documentation, including their e-mails, letters, bank statements, cancelled checks, and the like. Based on what you know, see if you can find *anything* that will give us a lead on either of these two cases? I'm particularly interested in information that ties Weston and Hayes together as well as something that might relate to a man and woman, possibly man and wife, who we believe are from the Middle East. You may be able to recognize them by their Middle Eastern names. Use this keyword list—it's the same one I gave to Dugan and O'Keeffe—as you go through the material to help identify portions of documents that will be of interest to us.

"With respect to Weston, pay particular attention to documents written or typed during the summer months, when this couple and their child is said to have visited him."

"And what are your plans?"

"While I wait for an evaluation of the forensic evidence we gathered in Lake George, particularly the fingerprint data, I'm going to pull Weston's calendars from the Evidence Room and go over them with a fine-tooth comb. I'll also check Hayes's evidence box for calendars and examine those as well. What I'll be looking for is anything that might tie the two men together as well as evidence of a bloodletting or vampire-related relationship with this couple of interest."

Alexa rose. "Got it. If there's something there, I'll find it."

"You know what? I might as well drive over to 1PP now. That way, I can give you a ride back to your office and pick up the evidence I need at the same time."

"I don't care what they say about you, Detective Martelli, you're a gentleman through and through."

■ *Theodore Jerome Cohen*

Twenty

While Martelli dug through Weston's evidence box for calendars, Beauvais retrieved and signed for all of the paper documentation she could find in Hayes's box. She and Martelli then exchanged boxes, and they repeated their searches for material. Fortuitously, Martelli was able to find calendars for 2009, 2010, and 2011 among the material taken from Hayes's apartment, giving him three years of overlap with the calendars retrieved from Weston's two residences.

"I'm going to work on these in my office, Lou," remarked Beauvais, as she signed for the evidence. "I'll return everything to custody before I leave tonight. Where will you be if I need you?"

"I'm going to work down here, over there," he said, pointing to a desk and chair as he signed for the calendars.

"Great. I'll let you know as soon as I have something. And if you find something noteworthy, give me a shout. It might save me some time."

"Will do."

Martelli took the calendars and made his way to the desk, which was located off to one side of the room. Taking off his suit coat, he hung it neatly on the back of the chair. Then, he sat down to begin looking through Weston's calendar for 2006, pen and paper at the ready.

The temptation to look at the page for July was too great, and he immediately turned to that month. He wasn't disappointed.

There it is . . . Wednesday, July 19th . . . and the name 'Mariam.' This is too good to be true, he thought.

He quickly grabbed the calendar for 2007. *Ah ha . . . they were there on July 17th . . . a Tuesday. Same woman's name. Damn. Why didn't he write down the name of the man?*

And 2008? He hurriedly turned the pages, finding the month of July. *There her name penciled in . . . a little later this year . . . Wednesday, the 23rd.*

He quickly checked the July pages in the calendars for 2009 and 2010, but found nothing. *This confirms what the neighbors said.*

Quickly turning to the calendar for 2011, he checked for an entry in July on the day before Weston's body was found. *Nothing! Which means Weston wasn't expecting him.*

Martelli scribbled the dates and the woman's name on the yellow pad to his right, and then dug into his suit coat pocket for his cell phone. His first call was to Dugan.

"Missy, add 'Mariam' to your keyword list. I certain that's the name of a woman who visited Weston at his lake home on several occasions. More importantly, I'm equally certain the man who accompanied her on those visits is our killer."

"And while you're at it, on the possibility that Mariam drives, run the name through DMV. Let's get a list of all the women in New York City with that first name. As I recall from my time in the Middle East, a variant on that name is 'Maryam,' with a 'y,' so use that spelling as well."

"Not a problem."

"Also, keep these dates in mind. July 19, 2006, July 17, 2007, and July 23, 2008. I'm not exactly sure of their significance, but they *are* important to this case."

"Got 'em, Lou. That could save us some time."

"Great. Now I need to call Alexa. Talk to you later."

He terminated the call and speed dialed Beauvais.

"Hey, Lou. Don't tell me you found something already."

"You know me . . . fastest guy in town."

"That's what all the women say."

"You've been spending too much time talking to Steph.

"In any event, be especially watchful for anything containing the name 'Mariam.' I don't have a last name, but there's no doubt in my mind she's the woman described by the neighbors as having visited Weston. And I'm just as sure that the man who accompanied her is our killer. Unfortunately, I don't have enough information to put out a BOLO for either of them.

"Oh, yeah, one last thing. Keep these dates in mind while you're going through all that material. July 19, 2006, July 17, 2007, and July 23, 2008. There were critical events that took place on those dates, and we need to link them to the evidence.

"Work your magic, darlin'."

"I'm on it, Lou."

Martelli put his cell phone on the table and returned to Weston's calendars. Starting on January 1, 2006, he methodically reviewed the entries for each date, progressing through the summer and into the fall. He found entries in November 2006 and 2007 marked 'Mariam,' and none after that. All of the other references in Weston's calendars referred to the more mundane aspects of his life . . . doctor's appointments, luncheon engagements with his daughter, appointments to have work performed on appliances, and the like.

107

A search of Hayes's calendars showed two entries with the name "Mariam.' The first was found in March, 2007. Martelli made a note of that. He continued on and into 2008.

Wait . . . what's this? There's an entry with the name 'Mariam' written in for November 11th. Hmmm . . . not just her name . . . it says 'At Mariam's.'

He looked at the notes he had made regarding Weston's calendars at the top of the sheet. *There it is . . . Wednesday, November 11th. It's a match. The three of them knew each other. I knew it!*

Martelli was ecstatic. He grabbed his cell phone and speed dialed Dugan's lab.

"Yes, Lou."

"Is Sean there yet?"

"Yes, he just arrived."

"Great . . . put me on speakerphone."

"Here you go."

"Good morning, Lou."

"Hey, Sean. Listen, guys, I just connected the dots . . . I found evidence that Weston, Hayes, and the woman who visited Weston in Lake George, who's referred to as 'Mariam,' knew each other. In fact, the three of them, and possibly others, were together on Wednesday, November 11, 2008 at Mariam's home or apartment, wherever that may be."

Sean let out a low whistle. "That's great work, Lou."

"And do we have news for you!"

"What's that?"

"Just before you called, Missy and I found another piece of the puzzle, though we're not sure where it fits."

Martelli could barely contain his excitement. "Lay it on me!"

"We just discovered an e-mail exchange between Weston and Hayes from 4 years ago. In it, Hayes asked Weston if someone named 'Felicia' had been able to find a book for him written by someone named Hearn."

"Go on!"

"Missy did a quick Internet search, and the author's full name, given the subject matter of interest—vampires—must be Patrick Lafcadio Hearn. Further, the book probably is *Stories and Studies of Strange Things,* which was published in 1903. It discusses the 'Nukekubi,' which are monsters found in Japanese folklore. Their heads are said to detach from their bodies, fly about in search of human prey, and attack their victims by closing in and biting them. It all ties together, Lou, because Hearn also was known by his Japanese name as Koizumi Yakumo."

"Hmmm . . . I wonder why Hayes would depend on this 'Felicia' woman to find the book. Perhaps she works in a library or used bookstore. What do you think, Sean?"

"Sounds reasonable. What do you think, Missy?"

"I don't know. But without a last name, we're pretty much dead in the water, Lou."

"Yeah, I know. But thanks, guys.

"Keep digging. There must be more in the material you have that can take this investigation to the next level. Meanwhile, I'm going to make arrangements to meet with Weston's daughter, and see if she can tell me anything."

Sean bent over to talk into the Dugan's speakerphone. "What about Hayes's relative?"

"He's in New Jersey. I got his contact information from Antonetti. I'll give him a call as well."

"Good luck, Lou."

■ *Theodore Jerome Cohen*

Twenty-one

"Thank you for meeting with me on such short notice, Miss Weston." Weston, single and in her 40s, was on leave from her job as a financial research assistant so that she would have time to address urgent matters pertaining to her father's estate.

"I know how distressing this entire situation must be for you, and I'll try to be as brief as I can. First, I want to express the Department's condolences on your loss. I also want to express our deepest appreciation for the cooperation you've given us. It's made our work so much easier. As well, we hope it will help us bring your father's killer to justice more quickly."

"I understand, Detective. It came as quite a shock to learn my father had been poisoned. And then, for someone to do what they did to his body in the sanctuary of the church . . . ." Her voice trailed off.

"What kind of relationship did you have with your father? That is, did you speak to or see him often?"

"We weren't close, if that's what you're asking. He was always very strict with me as a child. After my mother died—when I was in my teens—it got worse. He was forever sticking his nose in my business, to the point where I almost had no life of my own. I blame him for destroying several

111

good relationships I had with men. As a matter of fact, I never married.

"Fortunately, after college, I was able to get a good paying job in the Financial District. It's the only thing that saved me. By investing my money, I finally had enough in the bank to move out of his apartment when I was in my late-20s."

"I take it, then, you had very little contact with your father after that."

She nodded and looked as if she might begin to cry. Martelli waited.

"After I moved out, we saw each other only on Christmas Day . . . to exchange gifts. It was a family tradition."

She shrugged. "What can I say? I needed the emotional support it provided. At least my shrink encouraged me to continue the tradition on the possibility it might help to restore some balance in my life, family-wise."

"I understand. Please go on."

"Then, a few years ago, my father started reaching out to me. At first, it was just an occasional invitation for lunch. He'd make up some excuse that he was going to be downtown and wondered whether we might grab lunch together. This grew into a more frequent meetings—every month or so—especially in the spring and fall, for lunch or dinner."

"What did you talk about during those times?"

"It was mostly idle chatter . . . you know, the weather, local politics, and the like."

"Did he ever ask you about your life?"

"All the time. But he wasn't as intense about it as he was when I was younger. Still, he would ask what I was doing, if I was seeing anyone in particular, if I was serious about that person, and so forth."

"And, I assume, you asked questions about his personal life?"

"Well, nothing like the kinds of questions he asked me, that's for sure. I'd ask if he had been to see any Broadway plays, whether he had been traveling . . . things like that."

"Did you ever visit him at his summer home on Lake George?"

"No. Never. First, he never invited me to the lake, and second, I had no way of getting there. I don't own a car."

"Did he ever talk about his friends . . . people he knew either in New York City or Lake George?"

"Not really. Dad was a very private man. I think he stuck pretty much to himself. But he did talk about one of his next door neighbors at the lake, a man who borrowed things from him . . . I can't think of his name—"

"Arnold Braun?"

"Yes, that's him. Every time I saw my father, he would complain that Braun never returned the books my dad lent to him. My father said he was afraid they would get swallowed up in 'Braun's Dump,' as he called it, and that he'd never see them again.

"He also hated it when Braun came over to borrow tools. Dad used to say that anything Braun took with him disappeared into a black hole . . . that the man was a hoarder."

"Why didn't he just stop loaning things to him?"

"I asked him that. He said he was afraid that if he did, Braun wouldn't return what he already had."

Martelli shook his head and took a deep breath. "Let me ask you this, Miss Weston, was there ever a time when you thought your father might be behaving, say, a bit strangely?"

The question caught her off guard. "Whatever do you mean by that, Detective?"

113

"Well, did you ever find him acting uneasy or upset . . . not quite himself, as if something was bothering him?"

She thought for a moment.

"Well, there was this one time. I think it was around Christmas, 2008. We were having dinner. He seemed distracted."

"How so?"

"I don't know . . . I was saying something, making small talk, you know, and when I stopped, he seemed lost in his own thoughts. I asked if he was okay. He waved me off and said something like, 'Yes, yes, I'm fine. It's just that a couple I know has a child who's very ill.'"

"Did he happen to mention the name of the child or, perhaps, the name of the couple? For example, did he ever mention a woman by the name of Mariam?"

"No, he never mentioned any names. Who's Mariam?"

"She's a person of interest. By the way, did your father ever mention someone by the name of Byron Hayes?"

"No, I can't say he did? Did this Mr. Hayes know my father?"

"That's what we've been trying to determine."

Miss Weston nodded. "I see."

"So, as you were saying, your father seemed upset—"

Martelli was about to pursue the matter of the couple's child when his cell phone rang. He glanced at the screen and saw that it was Sergeant Adam Reynolds, NYPD CSU.

"Excuse me for a minute, Miss Weston, I must take this call."

"I understand, Detective."

"Yes, Adam."

"Lou, I just received the forensic results for the fingerprints taken both at Weston's apartment in Manhattan and at his cottage in Lake George. Sorry, buddy, but we've accounted for all of them. Nothing but Weston's and the super's at the apartment.

"At the cottage, we found the sheriff's prints as well as those of two deputies, the coroner, one firefighter, and the medic on various doorknobs as well as on objects in the front room and kitchen. We also found the next door neighbor's prints—"

"Braun's."

"Yeah, Braun's . . . we found his prints on the front window. He must have put his fingers on the window pane while peering into the house.

"Sorry, Lou . . . I wish I had better news for you."

"That's okay, Adam. I know you and your people did your best. Thanks for putting the rush on it, and please let everyone know how appreciative O'Keeffe and I are!"

"Thanks, Lou. I'll do that."

"Bye."

Martelli slipped his cell phone into his suit coat pocket and turned back to Weston.

"I apologize.

"So, as you were saying, your father seemed upset by the fact this couple's child was ill."

"Yes, he was so upset, in fact, that he finally said he'd take a rain check on coffee and dessert . . . that perhaps next month would be a better time to meet for that."

"Did you?"

"Meet? No. One month stretched into two, and then three. You know how it goes. Soon it was late spring, and time for him to drive to Lake George."

"Did you see him in the fall when he returned?"

"No, I saw him at Christmas. He seemed sad, and I thought, well, perhaps his friends' child had died. I didn't dare ask though."

"And after that?"

"The next time I saw him was in the spring of 2010, just before he left for Lake George. He seemed fine. He talked about how great it would be to get back to the lake, and how he was looking forward to just sitting in the sun and reading."

Martelli made notes as she spoke.

"What do you know about your father's reading habits?"

"Not much. I hadn't been to his apartment for many years, and as I said, I've never been to his lake home."

"Would you be surprised if I told you that your father had an extensive library of books on the subject of vampires?"

"So do most of the teenagers across the country, Detective. Or don't you keep up on current trends?"

"You're correct, of course. And I certainly can attest to the fact my daughter can hold her own with the best of them when it comes to discussing the *Twilight Saga*."

"Why, Detective Martelli, you surprise me. I wouldn't have guessed you had *heard* of the *Twilight Saga*, much less knew what it's about. And here I thought anyone over 25 was considered an old fuddy-duddy these days."

Martelli laughed. "I'm not quite 'shovel ready' yet, Miss Weston. But seriously, the books and other things in your father's library aren't the type of literature you're apt to find on a teenager's bookshelf. We found serious academic texts, archival literature, and even newspaper clippings on the subject of vampirism. There was one article, for example, from *The Telegraph* that cited Italian researchers who had unearthed what they believed to be the remains of a female vampire in Venice who had been buried with a brick between her jaws. This was done, apparently, to prevent her from feeding on victims of the plague that swept the city in the 16th century. Don't you find all of this in the least bit curious?"

"No, not really. Dad's interests spanned a broad range of genre, from fiction, to biographies, to history . . . you name it, he read it. I can't remember a time when dad *didn't* have a book, magazine, or newspaper in his hands. He even volunteered at the New York Public Library on 5th Avenue so he would have ready access to just about anything he wanted. Perhaps you should contact the people who worked with him . . . they probably could tell you more about his reading habits than anyone."

"That's an excellent suggestion, Miss Weston! Thank you, this has been most helpful. Here's my card. If anything comes to mind, please call me. You never know what might be important."

"I'll do that, Detective. And thank you for your good work. I sincerely appreciate what you're doing to solve my father's murder."

■ *Theodore Jerome Cohen*

Twenty-two

'**Mr.** Evans, this is Detective Louis Martelli of the New York Police Department. Your wife gave me your work number. I apologize for calling you at the office, but this is a matter of some urgency."

"No problem, Detective. Just give me a moment, if you would, please. My associate was about to leave. I'll see him to the door."

Martelli heard Evans put him on hold. *Well, at least there's some pleasant music to keep me—*

"Here I am, Detective. How may I help you?"

"I understand you're Byron Hayes's only living relative, is that correct?"

"Yes, that's right."

"When's the last time you saw your uncle?"

"Let's see . . . it was about two months before he was killed."

"That would have been in early 2010, then."

"Yes, in March."

"Okay, can you tell me a little about that meeting?"

"Well, I had to be in the city for a conference and trade show—I work in the pharmaceutical industry—so I thought I'd ring him up and see if he wanted to have lunch. I hadn't

119

seen him in several years, and I thought, 'What the hell, he's family.'"

"So, where did you two meet?"

"Well, he lived on the upper West Side, just off Riverside Drive, on 102nd. So I jumped on the Uptown-1 around 11:30 that morning and met him at Henry's . . . you know, the bistro at Broadway and 105th."

"Yes, I know the place."

"Great place, wonderful food!"

"How did he look?"

"Not well. I hadn't seen him for some time, as I said, but frankly, I was a little shocked."

"What do you mean?"

"Well, he looked pale and drawn. And he appeared to have lost some weight. I thought it might simply be the result of his getting older, not that he was *that* old . . . I think he was in his 50s, as I recall. But he just didn't look as healthy as I remembered him being the last time I saw him."

"What was his demeanor? Was he excited to see you?"

"He seemed pleased, but still, his response was muted. I don't know . . . he just didn't seem, for lack of a better word, 'happy.'"

"What did you talk about?"

"I did most of the talking, Detective. I brought him up to speed on my family—you know, my wife and two children—the job, what we were planning to do that year for our summer vacation, things like that."

"And what did *he* talk about?"

"Not much. I asked him how his job was going—he worked as a salesman for a wholesale wine and liquor distributor in the city, one that primarily served the restaurant trade—and he said sales were picking up. He said that among other trends in the industry, people were switching from beer to wine, so their year-over-year revenues were increasing at the same time their profit margins were expanding."

"Sounds like he should have been extremely happy."

"You would think so."

"Did he say anything about his friends or acquaintances?"

"Not that I recall."

"How about a man by the name of Phillip Weston . . . did that gentleman's name come up in conversation?"

"No, I'm sure of that."

"How about a woman by the name of Mariam?"

"Who?"

"Mariam."

"No, I would have remembered that. Our secretary has a 2-year-old daughter by the name of Mary Ann. I would have remembered him mentioning the other name . . . what was it again?"

"Mariam."

"No, I'm absolutely positive he didn't mention anyone by that name."

"Mr. Evans, can you tell me anything about the funeral service for your late uncle? I assume you were in attendance."

"Oh, yes, we took a New Jersey Transit train out of Princeton Junction straight into Penn Station. The service was held at St. Catherine's in Manhattan."

"How long, would you say, the body was available for viewing in the sanctuary before the service began?"

"Oh, maybe 30 minutes, maybe a little longer."

"Were there many mourners?"

"Not really . . . perhaps twenty or so."

"I know this might sound funny, but did you notice anything strange about one or more of the people paying their last respects?"

Evans did not respond immediately.

"Mr. Evans?"

"I'm still here, Detective. You know, I hadn't given it much thought. But now that you mention it, I recall seeing a priest enter the sanctuary from the back of the church, approach the coffin, appear to pray over the body, and then leave via the back door. At the time I didn't think much about it, but on hindsight, it *does* seem a bit unusual. I mean, my uncle was not a religious person. So why would a man of the cloth, other than the priest who would officiate at his funeral, pay special attention to him?"

"By any chance, was the man dressed in a long robe and wearing a black, low-crowned, wide-brimmed ecclesiastical hat?"

"Yes, that's the person. How did you know?"

"A person fitting that description was seen at the funeral of someone who we think may have known your uncle. We're just trying to establish the relationship among the three."

"Oh, I understand. Look, Detective Martelli, I'm sorry, but I'm going to have to cut this short. I have a meeting with my boss in 5 minutes, and I need to grab some files and get down the hall to her office. Is there anything else I can do for you right now?"

"No, Mr. Evans. You've been most helpful."

Martelli provided the man with his cell phone number and asked him to call, day or night, if he remembered anything more about the meeting with his uncle or his uncle's funeral, no matter how inconsequential he thought it might be.

"Count on me, Detective. If anything comes to mind, I'll call you immediately."

■ *Theodore Jerome Cohen*

Twenty-three

'Well, if this isn't a pleasant surprise." Martelli had just walked into his office in the First Precinct, where Beauvais, deeply engrossed in the final analysis of a stack of cancelled checks, sat waiting for him. It was 6:30 AM, well before many members of the day staff had arrived.

"I thought I'd drop by and show you what I had before running uptown and visiting with my mother for a few minutes."

"Care for some coffee?"

"Sure. You buying?"

"Of course. It'll take me just be a minute to run to the corner. How do you like yours?"

"Cream and sugar, please."

"All right. Stand by."

He disappeared down the hall, and made his way up the stairs, through the front door, and down the street to the coffee shop. A crowd was just beginning to form, but in 15 minutes, he was back in the precinct.

"Here you go . . . nice and hot."

"Thanks, Lou. You know, while you were gone, I finished culling through the last of the cancelled checks from Weston's account. I've been through everything for both men . . . their bank statements, cancelled checks, what few e-mails they printed, and whatever else I found in the evidence boxes, and—"

"And?"

"And if these men knew each other, there is absolutely nothing here that links them together."

"You're sure."

"Positive. On the basis of these data, you're looking at two completely separate lives . . . lives that never intersected."

"Great!" he said, facetiously. "We know from other evidence they almost certainly knew each other because they both knew a woman whose name is 'Mariam' and they both were scheduled to be with this 'Mariam' on the same day in the fall of 2008 . . . on Wednesday, November 11th, to be exact. But what I *really* was hoping you could give me is this 'Mariam's' last name, or the name of her husband, or, perhaps, the name of her daughter."

Martelli took a deep breath and let the air out slowly. "Damn! I guess that lead just petered out."

"Well, I wouldn't throw the towel in quite yet, Lou."

"What do you mean?"

"I found checks signed by Weston that were dated July 19, 2006, July 17, 2007, and July 23, 2008. The notation on each one reads 'Happy Birthday.' The amount is the same on all three checks . . . $20."

"Come on, you're killing me! Who were they made out to?"

"Someone named 'Salomea.'"

"That must be the daughter's name."

"It's beautiful, Lou."

"I know. Did anyone fill in a last name on the front of the checks?"

"No, all three contain just the first name."

"What about the backs? Who cashed them? How were their countersigned?"

"That's just it . . . from the handwriting, it looks like the child printed her first name using all capital letters. Whoever cashed them, and it probably was a friend, must have simply given her cash."

"Can I see them?"

"Sure, knock yourself out." She handed him the three checks.

"All three of these were processed by a check cashing corporation known then as Kwik-Kash4UNYC, LLC."

Martelli turned to his computer and did a Google search for the company. "Nothing in this area operating under that name today. Those outfits come and go as fast as I change my underwear, so I'm not surprised this one's no longer in business, at least not under that name."

"But wouldn't they have had a business license?"

"Right you are!" Martelli picked up his telephone handset and punched Missy Dugan's extension into the keypad.

"Lou! I was just about to call you. We found this 'Felicia' woman!"

Dugan sounded extremely excited. Martelli could hear O'Keeffe in the background saying something to her, but he could not make it out.

"What did Sean say?"

"He said he can't believe what we just found."

"What is it?"

"An e-mail dated November 9, 2008, from someone named Felicia Duval, who apparently works at the New York Public Library—that's the last part of her e-mail address . . . you know, 'nypl.org'—asking Weston, and I paraphrase, 'for a ride to Mariam's apartment for their gathering on Wednesday night, November 11, 2008.'"

"What was his response?"

"He said he would pick her up at 7 PM, at her place. But there's nothing else of use that we could find."

"Did you do a search for other e-mails from Duval?"

"Yes, there was none."

"This could be the break we've been waiting for. Ask Sean to jump in his car and pick me up. I want to drive over to the library at Fifth Avenue and 42nd Street, and see if we can catch her. At the least, we might be able to learn something that will help us.

"And Missy, dig up what you can for us regarding where Duval lives, her home telephone number, and so forth, and send it to my cell phone. We may need it if we can't learn anything while we're at the library."

Martelli heard Dugan relay his message to O'Keeffe.

"Sean says to tell you he's leaving now. He'll pick you up in front of the precinct. And I'll get you the information you need as soon as I can."

"Great. While Sean is on the way over here, do me a favor. See if you can find a company called Kwik-Kash4UNYC, LLC. It was in the check cashing business between 2006 and 2008 . . . maybe 2009, as well. I can't find a current listing for them."

"Stand by."

Martelli covered his phone and whispered to Beauvais. "She's checking now."

"Found 'em, Lou. They apparently ceased operations in 2009. At least no city license was issued to a 'Kwik-Kash4UNYC, LLC' for 2010 and beyond."

"Who's listed as the owner on the city business license for 2009?"

"Let's see . . . ah, here it is. Faraz Tehrani."

"Terrific. Fax me a copy of the license, would you? It should contain Tehrani's home address. I need to pay him a visit."

"One more thing, Lou . . . regarding that search you asked me to do on women in New York City with the name 'Mariam.'"

"Yeah?"

"There are 11,568 women in Manhattan alone with that first name or the variant you gave me. I think you're going to need a wee bit more information before we can locate your suspect."

"Man, ain't that the truth. Thanks, darlin'."

"Don't mention it."

"And thank *you,* Alexa. You done good!"

■ *Theodore Jerome Cohen*

Twenty-four

'**A**re you okay, Lou?" O'Keeffe had just picked up his partner in front of the First Precinct, as Martelli had requested. O'Keeffe could see his partner looked tired and drawn. There were dark circles under his eyes, and he looked as if he were in need of a good night's sleep. Clearly, the Weston and Hayes cases were taking their toll on the precinct's lead detective.

"I'll be all right. It's just that right now, I'm running on fumes. I don't think I've slept 7 hours in the last 2 days."

O'Keeffe nodded. "I can understand that. These cases are puzzling. Add the macabre element of vampirism, and it's enough to give you nightmares."

"Which is exactly what it's doing."

"Damn it, Lou, are you having them again? I thought you finally were able to put them behind you and move on . . . away from the crash in Iraq."

"I can't shake it, Sean. I can't put the crash out of my mind. It's bad enough I have to relive my attempts to rescue the pilots over and over again in my sleep. But now, because of these cases, I see the pilot and copilot reaching out to me from their graves, beckoning me toward them . . . calling for me to join them. I no sooner fall asleep than I wake up screaming, with the sheets drenched in sweat. Steph is so gentle and patient, but she's not getting much sleep, either. It's rough."

The men drove on, neither saying anything for several minutes.

"Do you believe in God, Sean?"

"Not really. I used to when I was a kid . . . when my aunt took me to church on Sunday mornings. But as I grew older, I drifted away from the Church. You?"

"Maybe?"

"Is that a 'definite maybe,' or is there some wiggle room there?"

Martelli laughed. "I don't know. It's hard to have faith in *anything* these days. Look at what's happening around the world on a daily basis . . . the killings and other crimes against humanity, many involving religious and ethnic cleansing."

O'Keeffe drove on, letting his partner sort out his thoughts.

It did not take long before Martelli broke the silence. "And on a larger scale, what's the Grand Scheme? What's the purpose of Life? What's the purpose of *my* life? At times, it just seems all so futile. Solve one case, another takes its place. It's like our country has lost its 'national conscience.' No one plays by the rules anymore. And I begin to wonder. Are we—you and me—being played for chumps by the elite?

"No matter how hard we work, it seems like we're slipping backwards. Crime is on the rise, criminals are back on the street before you and I finish their paperwork, enforcement at the federal level, especially of 'white collar' crimes, is a joke, and I ask myself . . . is this God's plan for the Universe? I mean, is it His intent that everything dissolves into chaos, and that in the end, mankind destroys itself?"

O'Keeffe just shook his head. "Don't look to me for the answers, Lou."

Martelli laughed. "I don't know that *anyone* has the answers, my friend."

O'Keeffe pulled into a No Parking zone in front of the New York Public Library at Fifth Avenue and 42nd Street and turned on the car's flashers. "Let's go. No rest for the weary."

■ *Theodore Jerome Cohen*

Twenty-five

The men made their way into the library and to the main desk. A young woman, Sarah Henry, by name, greeted them and asked how she might be of service. She was slightly taken aback when Martelli and O'Keeffe identified themselves as NYPD detectives and asked to see the library's administrator.

"Our administrator is Mrs. Irene Collins, Detectives. Her office is down this hallway . . . room 107. She has asked to have all visitors announced, so if you wouldn't mine giving me a minute, I'll give her a call."

Henry picked up her phone and dialed the administrator's extension.

"Mrs. Collins, I have two detectives from the New York Police Department at the front desk. They have asked to speak with you."

"Please send them down, Sarah."

Henry replaced her handset on the console, and turned to the men. "You may go to her office, gentlemen. Again, it's room 107." She pointed to the hallway on her right.

Martelli nodded. "Thank you, Miss Henry."

Collins was standing in her doorway when Martelli and O'Keeffe reached her office. "Won't you come in, gentlemen? Please have a seat."

Both men sat and presented their badges and official identification cards.

"How may I be of service to the police?"

Martelli took the lead. "Mrs. Collins, we need to talk with one of your employees regarding a matter of interest in two cases we're working."

"And who would that be, Detective Martelli?"

"Felicia Duval, ma'am."

"Felicia. Ah, yes . . . she works in Technical Services, primarily Cataloging. Let me call and see if she's in."

Collins picked up her phone and dialed Duval's extension. There was no answer.

"That's strange. She's usually in her office by now. Let me call her supervisor, Don Jamison."

She dialed Jamison's extension.

"Don, Irene here."

"Hi, Irene. How's everything?"

"Fine. Listen, I need to speak with Felicia, but apparently, she's out of her office. Have you seen her today?"

"Funny you should ask. She didn't come in this morning. And she wasn't in yesterday, either. I tried calling her apartment an hour ago, but there was no answer. This isn't like her . . . she's always so punctual. There's never been a time when she didn't let me know if she was going to be late, much less take a day off. I hope nothing's wrong."

"Let's hope not, Don. Thanks."

Collins placed her telephone handset on the console and looked up.

Martelli raised his eyebrows. "That didn't sound good."

"No, it didn't, Detective."

"Mrs. Collins, could I ask you for Miss Duval's home address and telephone number, please. Perhaps we should meet with her at her apartment."

"Of course, Detective."

She quickly retrieved Duval's personal information from the library's database, made a note of the data Martelli had requested on a piece of notepaper, and handed it to him.

"I hope she's not in any kind of trouble, Detective."

"I hope not, Mrs. Collins.

"And thank you for your time. We'll let ourselves out."

■ *Theodore Jerome Cohen*

Twenty-six

It was shortly after 1 PM by the time Martelli and O'Keeffe made their way to the Upper West Side and Duval's apartment on West End Avenue. On the way, they grabbed lunch from a street vendor, which did neither of their stomachs good.

"What are you looking for," asked O'Keeffe, when he observed Martelli rifling through his glove box.

"Don't you have anything for an upset stomach? That hotdog was *the* absolute worst thing I've ever eaten."

"It wasn't the hotdog, Lou . . . it was the sauerkraut."

"Whatever it was, my stomach is in an uproar!"

"There should be some Pepto Bismol tablets in there . . . on the left. Do you see them?"

"Yeah, here they are. Do you want two?"

"You bet. Thanks."

Sean parked his *Crown Vic* in the 'signed' Loading Zone to the front of Duval's apartment building, and the men went into the lobby. There was no doorman, and entry was by key only.

Martelli started pushing buttons.

Almost immediately, an elderly man responded on the intercom.

"Yes. Who is it?"

"Rapid Delivery . . . package for you."

139

The buzzer sounded. Martelli pulled the door open, and he and O'Keeffe walked into the building and up to the 4th floor.

"Duval's apartment is 4E, Sean."

The men walk toward the front of the building, which overlooked West End Avenue. Duval's apartment was the last one on the left.

Martelli was just about to knock on the door when it hit him.

"Do you smell that?"

"Oh, yeah . . . it's unmistakable."

The men took out handkerchiefs, covered their mouths and noses, backed away from the door, and retreated 20 feet down the hall. At that point, Martelli grabbed the Motorola MTX8000 police-fire two-way radio from his waist and keyed up the transmitter.

"First Squad to Central."

"Go to First Squad."

Martelli immediately reported a possible Code 10-64Q—Quality of Life Incident-Foul Odor—and Code 10-10—Possible Crime—at Duval's address, following by a request for a black and white backup accompanied by a fire and rescue unit.

"10-4, First Squad."

"Sean, find the super and get him up here. We're going to need him to open the door when fire and rescue arrive. While you're gone, I'm going to talk with anyone I can find at home on this floor. Perhaps someone heard or saw something. We'll have to wait on talking with the people in the apartment across from Duval's until we can get rid of the odor."

"Got it. I'll be right back."

While Sean searched for the super, Martelli met with several of Duval's neighbors. No one recalled seeing her in the last two days. Nor did any of her neighbors remember seeing anyone in the hallway other than residents during that time.

It took O'Keeffe almost 10 minutes to find the super, who he immediately escorted to the 4th floor. Within minutes of their joining Martelli, additional police officers as well as fire and rescue personnel arrived and made their way to Duval's apartment.

Martelli, who already had put on latex gloves, asked the super to unlock the door but not to touch the knob.

"I'll open the door once you unlock it. After that, please step back. One thing you could do for me, though, is grab the surveillance tapes containing the video from cameras in the front lobby, stairwells, and this floor. I want everything recorded during the last three days. If you would, put them in a box and bring them here. I'll need them for evidence."

The super, his nose and mouth covered with a handkerchief, shook his head. "I wish I could do that, Detective, but our security system hasn't been working for over a week. I haven't been able to get anyone over here even to look at it."

Martelli threw him a disgusted look.

The super inserted a key in the door's deadbolt lock and turned it. Then, he inserted another key in the door knob's lock and stepped back. Carefully, Martelli turned the key and pushed the apartment door open.

■ *Theodore Jerome Cohen*

Twenty-seven

The scene before them was horrific. The stench was overwhelming. Duval's body lay naked on the living room floor, an oak stake driven through her heart. Her head lay 5 feet from her body, eyes staring blankly at the ceiling. A clove of garlic protruded from the mouth.

Martelli and O'Keeffe immediately retreated to the hallway, where Martelli put in a call for assistance from CSU and Deputy Coroner Antonetti. Meanwhile, two firemen, wearing gasmasks, opened windows in the apartment and positioned high-capacity fans to exhaust the foul air.

Martelli slumped to the rug in the hallway and put his head in his hands.

"Man, this is just about as bad as it gets, Sean."

O'Keeffe sat beside him. "I'll say. I can't remember seeing anything like this since leaving Iraq."

Martelli turned and looked at him. "At least the perp left the body behind."

"Yeah. Thanks for small favors! As I recall, you never found anything but the heads of the two men murdered in New York last year on that case involving a breast cancer drug the FDA refused to approve."

Martelli nodded. "That's right. And the DC police only found the head and one hand of the man murdered in Washington on the same case."

"What makes a person do something like this?"

"I wish I knew. But I can tell you this . . . when we have the answer to that question, we'll be a long way down the path toward solving this case."

Eleven minutes passed before Antonetti and two NYPD CSU personnel arrived on the scene. Martelli and O'Keeffe stood to meet them.

"I understand I'm here by personal invitation, Louis. To what do I owe the honor?"

"Another vampire slaying, my friend. It's pretty gruesome. But at least we have the whole body, albeit in two pieces."

By now the air in the apartment was reasonably clear of odors, and Martelli, O'Keeffe, Antonetti, and the CSU personnel could begin working the crime scene. Antonetti kneeled down beside the body, examined it, and took its temperature.

"As best I can tell, Louis, she was killed about 40 hours ago, plus or minus."

He lifted her hands one by one, turned them over, and checked under her fingernails.

"She doesn't appear to have struggled. I suspect she knew her killer."

Sean looked at the body. "Any signs she was raped? Perhaps we could get a DNA sample?"

"I don't see any outward signs of forced sexual entry, but we'll have to wait until I can get her into the morgue and run some tests."

"And what's that bruise on her arm, Doc?"

Antonetti looked closely at Duval's right arm.

"Hmmm . . . that's a hematoma. It would appear someone recently drew blood from this young lady. Judging from the bloodstains around the point where the needle entered her arm, it was done just before she was killed.

"Look, why don't you and Sean work with the CSU personnel while I prepare the head and body for conveyance to the morgue?"

"Good idea, Michael.

"Come on, Sean. Bag and tag anything that might help us. We don't have much time to crack this case. If what happened here leaks to the press, our lives will become a living hell."

■ *Theodore Jerome Cohen*

Twenty-eight

It was after 7 PM when CSU finished their work at Duval's apartment and departed with the evidence collected. Antonetti had left the apartment hours earlier with the body, shortly after fire and rescue personnel left the scene. At one point during the afternoon, O'Keeffe stepped out to question the tenant in the apartment across from Duval's. The resident provided no useful information. Now, as Martelli and O'Keeffe were leaving, the police were preparing to seal the apartment and mark it as a crime scene.

"Come on, Lou. I'm taking you home. You look exhausted, and there's nothing more we can do tonight. The evidence won't be available for anyone to review until tomorrow morning, and frankly, you look like you're just about to keel over. You need a good meal, a sedative, and a good night's sleep . . . in that order. And I'm not taking 'no' for an answer!"

"Thanks, Sean. I know you're right. If I could keep my eyes open, I'd insist on you driving us to Tehrani's residence. We need to talk with him as soon as possible regarding the checks he cashed for Mariam's little girl . . . at least we have reason to believe it's her child."

"Look, Lou . . . I'll pick you up at your house tomorrow morning at 7:30, and then, we can drive straight to Tehrani's home from your place. You told me the guy lives in Brooklyn,

147

right? So, it couldn't be more convenient. We'll get there before 8 AM, giving us a good shot at catching him or someone who'll know where he is."

"All right. I'll be ready when you arrive. But not a word of what we talked about to Steph. She's already worried enough. If she asks any questions when you drop me off, I'm just going to say we had to drop my car at the Motor Pool, and that you'll be picking me up in the morning."

"And you really think that'll work, don't you?"

"No, but she'll understand. And it'll save you from being subjected to the third degree!"

Twenty-nine

Martelli slid into his partner's car without so much as rippling the surface of the coffee in his mug. "Hey, Sean. How'd you sleep last night?"

"The question is not how *I* slept, but how *you* slept."

"Like a baby. Until Hanlon started shouting in my ear at 6 this morning."

"Hanlon? What the hell set *him* off?"

"An article in the *Post* about the Duval murder. He's absolutely convinced that someone in 1PP leaked the story of the beheading to the paper . . . big spread on the front page this morning about it being some kind of ritual slaying. Fortunately, not enough information was made available to the paper to link it to the other cases we're working. But the fact the story got out at all, and the way it was presented, means the press'll soon be breathing down our necks."

"What's Hanlon going to do about it?"

"Well, he said he needs to buy us time, and fast. And because he has a good idea who leaked the story, he said he's going to kill two birds with one stone."

"What the hell does *that* mean?"

"Well, he's going to tell that person—"

"Who is it, Lou?"

"I asked, but he refused to tell me. Anyway, he's going to tell the guy that the murder is linked to the Cassidy slaying, which occurred in 2005."

"I remember that case. It's cold now. As I recall, a young woman was found beheaded in her apartment on the Upper East Side, with strange demonic symbols carved in her torso. The perp was never caught."

Martelli took a sip of coffee. "That's the one. Hanlon's going to say the Duval murder *might* be the work of the same person, and his people are looking into that possibility as a lead."

"Ah, I get it. And if that information turns up in the *Post* within a day or so—attributed, of course, to a source 'close to the investigation who is not authorized to speak on the record'—Hanlon will have his leaker *and* the heat will be off of us because the press will be off on a wild goose chase."

"Right."

"I sure wouldn't want to be the guy who leaked the information to the press, Lou. Hanlon will cut his balls off!"

"I know. Do you remember what he did to that cop, what was his name, oh yeah, Thompson 2 years ago?"

"You mean the undercover narc assigned to the First Precinct who was selling drugs out of his car?"

"One and the same. When a snitch came to Hanlon and reported what was going on, the captain set up a sting that not only caught Thompson, but two other cops as well. All three lost their badges and pensions."

Sean shook his head. "I thought for sure the union was going to throw a shitfit, but nothing happened."

"Actually, the union *did* attempt to reverse those terminations. A high-ranking union boss came to see Hanlon the day before the three officers were to be dismissed. I know because I was in the office the day the two men met. The union guy looked like he didn't have to answer to or take crap from anyone . . . a big bear of a man who probably got his start in local politics and fought his way up the union hierarchy until he now sat near the top. You could almost see steam coming out of his ears.

"Anyway, he and Hanlon met for 5 minutes before the captain's door flew open and the guy hightailed it out of there without saying so much as a 'fuck you and the horse you rode in on!' I don't know what Hanlon said or showed to him—maybe some pornographic pictures of the guy's wife with another man—but that was the end of it. I'll tell you this, Sean, don't you ever, *ever* get on Hanlon's Shit List. He'll make you wish you were never born."

O'Keeffe started to chuckle.

"What's so funny, Sean?"

"Oh, I was just wondering who Hanlon answers to. I mean, everyone has to answer to somebody. I know, I know. Hanlon *reports* to Commissioner Fields. But I mean, who does he *answer* to? Who calls the tune in the captain's life?"

Martelli laughed. "That's easy. Mrs. Hanlon!"

The men roared. When the laughter subsided, Martelli pulled out the piece of paper on which he had written Tehrani's address and handed it to O'Keeffe.

O'Keeffe glanced at it. "It's not far from here, Lou . . . perhaps 10 minutes. Buckle up. My driving, of course, is impeccable, but I can't vouch for the other idiots on the road."

"Yeah, I know," Martelli deadpanned, "like someone who might drive 105 miles an hour on an Interstate zoned for 65."

Martelli latched his belt as O'Keeffe pulled away from the curb. Traffic was building with the morning rush hour, but by sticking to the side streets, the trip to the Tehrani residence took less than 15 minutes. While O'Keeffe drove, Martelli made two phone calls.

"Missy. Martelli."

"Hey, Lou. I understand from Antonetti that you had one hellava day yesterday. Are you okay?"

"Yeah, I'll survive. I've been through worse. Not getting enough sleep was the killer.

"Listen, CSU picked up a ton of stuff from that woman's apartment. Her name was Duval. So, first things first. Go back and search the Weston and Hayes digital media for anything containing the keyword 'Duval.'"

"All right."

"Then, go to the Evidence Room and pull Duval's electronic media. You know the drill. I'm particularly interested in anything that pertains to Weston and Hayes as well as to the dates I cited earlier. Oh, yes, watch especially for references to 'Mariam.' Sean and I are convinced she's the key to unraveling these cases. Let me know as soon as you have something."

"I will. Supporting you is our Number One Priority, by direction of the Commissioner."

"I know I can count on you. To save me time, would you get ahold of Alexa, and ask her to run the traps on the bank statements, checkbooks, checks, and other material CSU pulled from the Duval apartment?"

"I'll leave a message for her as soon as we hang up."

"Thanks. Oh, by the way, we have no surveillance video from Duval's apartment building . . . the system hasn't worked for over a week."

"Well, that's a big help! Do I smell a lawsuit by Duval's family?"

"Wouldn't surprise me. I'll catch up with you later."

Martelli terminated the call and speed dialed Sergeant Reynolds at CSU.

"CSU, Sergeant Reynolds."

"Adam. Martelli."

"Hi, Lou. Wow, my people told me about the scene in that apartment on West End Avenue yesterday. That was unbelievable! What kind of person does that? It's savage."

"You need to get out from behind that desk and come with me into the field. You have no idea how depraved some people are."

"Oh, I have no illusions, believe me . . . I see enough just looking at the pictures that cross my desk.

"So, how can I help you this morning?"

"Regarding the vic whose body we found yesterday . . . she worked at the New York Public Library on 5th Avenue. Could you get a court order to search her office and then, send two CSIs over there to do a complete workup?"

"Absolutely."

"We'll also need a court order for her office e-mail. I think we should grab everything she sent or received over the last 5 years. It should be on the library's server."

"Can do." He laughed. "My people will pull everything but the furniture out of the place before we leave."

"That's what I want . . . everything but the kitchen sink."

"Consider it done."

"Thanks, Adam."

O'Keeffe pulled to the curb and parked. The men got out of the car and walked up the steps to the front door of the home at the address on the Kwik-Kash4UNYC, LLC business license Dugan had found.

O'Keeffe rang the doorbell. It took several minutes before a woman finally opened the door.

"Yes, may I help you?"

Martelli displayed his badge. "I'm Detective Louis Martelli, NYPD. This is Detective Sean O'Keeffe. Is Mr. Faraz Tehrani in?"

"Mr. Tehrani is dead, Detectives. He was my husband. He died just before Christmas, 2009. Perhaps I can help you."

"May we come in, Mrs. Tehrani?"

"Certainly, please do."

The men entered the modest home in an older part of Brooklyn.

"May I get you something to drink . . . coffee, perhaps?"

"None for me, thanks," answered Martelli.

"Just a glass of cold water, if you please," responded O'Keeffe.

"I'll be right back."

She returned shortly with a glass of cold water containing a slice of lemon, which she handed to O'Keeffe.

"Now, please go on."

Martelli was the first to speak. "Our condolences on the loss of your husband, Mrs. Tehrani. If it's not too upsetting, could you tell us, please, what was the cause of his death?"

"He died of a massive heart attack. Which was surprising, Detective, because he had just had his annual physical in November, and his doctor—"

"Who would that be?"

"Dr. Kourosh Jobrani. His office is on Atlantic."

"Thanks."

Martelli made a note of Jobrani and his location.

"His doctor said he was in excellent health. All his tests came back in the normal range, though the doctor wanted him to take iron supplements, for some reason. But other than that, everything appeared to be normal."

"Did you husband seem upset about anything before he died?"

"I don't understand?"

"Did anything happen to him or to friends of his that might have upset him or might have caused him concern in the months before he passed away?"

She thought for a minute.

"I can't think of anything, Detective."

Martelli pressed on.

"Your husband ran a check cashing business in Manhattan, correct?"

"Oh, yes. I worked with him. We were very successful."

"In the course of your work, did you ever cash checks for a little girl who goes by the name 'Salomea?'"

Mrs. Tehrani's face turned ashen. She put her hands to her cheeks. "Oh, my God!"

Then, without warning, she burst into tears. O'Keeffe pulled a handkerchief from his suit coat pocket and handed it to her. The men waited while she dabbed her eyes and composed herself.

"Such a beautiful child, but so pale. And to die so young."

The men exchanged glances.

Martelli shifted forward in his chair. "When did she die, Mrs. Tehrani?"

"I'm not sure, Detective. I only saw her two, maybe three times. The last time was in 2008, when she came into our business with her mother . . . at least I think it was her mother. That would have been some time in August."

"Do you happen to remember the mother's name?"

"It's not a matter of remembering her name . . . my husband never called her by name or said who she was."

"Well, what would happen when the child's mother—at least we think it was her mother—brought the girl into your establishment?"

"My husband would greet her with open arms, say something like 'Come here, my sweet child,' ask her to write her name on the back of a check someone had given her for her birthday—she was so proud of how beautifully she could write her name—hand her the money and a piece of candy, and then, the child and woman would leave."

"So, how do you know the little girl died?"

"One day, early in 2009, we were in the shop and a customer came in and mentioned that the little girl had passed away. He referred to her by her family's last name. I'm trying to remember it now. It's the same as a town in Iran, of course, but with an 'i' attached at the end."

Martelli turned to O'Keeffe. "Well, we both know a little about Iranian names based on the time we spent in that part of the world."

"You bet, Lou. Until relatively recently, the Iranian people didn't use family names. The naming traditions were more like the traditional Arabic names in that they reflected the names of the person's ancestors. Approximately 50 years ago, the elder Shah decided that all families should choose a family name. Many chose names relating to the city or town in which they lived by simply adding the letter 'i' to the name of the city or town."

"That's *exactly* how most of us got our names, Detective."

Martelli pressed on. "So, Mrs. Tehrani, please think back. Do you recall the name your customer used when he told you of the little girl's death?"

The woman turned her head and pursed her lips. It was clear that she wanted to be as helpful as possible.

"I think it began with an 'H' . . . perhaps Habibi or Harandi. Maybe even Hemmati, Detective."

"Thank you. Please excuse me a minute."

156

Martelli stood and walked to the other side of the room. While O'Keeffe and Mrs. Tehrani continued to make small talk, Martelli speed-dialed Dugan.

"Yes, Lou."

"I need you to do a search for a death certificate."

"Okay . . . what's the name?"

"The first name is Salomea." He spelled the name phonetically for her.

"Okay, I've entered it into the appropriate window. What's the surname?"

"I hope it's one of the following three: Habibi, Harandi, or Hemmati."

"Spell the last one phonetically for me, please."

Martelli spelled the name 'Hemmati' phonetically.

"Okay, if you can give me the year, this should go pretty fast."

"It was either 2008 or 2009."

"Okay, stand by."

Fifteen seconds passed.

"Bingo!"

"You found it?"

"Yep. Salomea Harandi, born July 5, 2002, died January 3, 2009."

"What was the cause of death?"

"Let's see . . . something called 'thalassemia major.'"

"Terrific. Now, go to *The New York Times* archives and pull the obituary."

"Hold one.

"Got it."

"How does it read?"

"'Salomea Harandi of Brooklyn passed away on Tuesday, January 3, 2009, at home after a lengthy and courageous battle with thalassemia major. She was 6.'

"'Born in Brooklyn, she—'"

"Skip to where they name the surviving members of her family."

"'She will be greatly missed by her mother and father, Mariam and Jafar Harandi. She is also—'"

"That's it! That's the information I'm missing for a BOLO. By the way, how is 'Mariam' spelled . . . with an 'i' or a 'y'?"

"With an 'i'"

"Please send me a copy of the death certificate and the obit in an e-mail, Missy. We'll still need you and Alexa to continue your searches for data in this case if for no other reason than the ADA will need anything you find for court proceedings. But this is what we need right now to search for the perp."

"Good luck, Lou. And please be careful. Remember what happened the last time you got a little too close to the killer, and he took you by surprise!"

"I still have a scar on the back of my head to remind me, darlin'."

Martelli returned to where O'Keeffe and Mrs. Tehrani were talking.

"Mrs. Tehrani, you'll have to excuse us. Something has come up. Detective O'Keeffe and I must regrettably leave for another appointment. You've been most kind to take the time to speak with us this morning. Here's my card— Detective O'Keeffe will give you his as well. If you should remember anything about the child and her mother, please call us."

"I'll do that, Detective. I hope I've been of some assistance to you."

"More than you realize, ma'am."

Martelli and O'Keeffe bid her goodbye, and returned to O'Keeffe's *Crown Vic.*

"What was that all about?"

"I think we now know the name of the killer!"

"Who?"

"A man by the name of Jafar Harandi."

Martelli picked the microphone clipped to the car's dashboard and keyed up the radio transmitter in the trunk.

"First Squad to Central."

"Go to First Squad."

"10-10 on the following person wanted in connection with multiple homicide investigations, Jafar Harandi, presumed US citizen of Iranian descent, last known residence, Brooklyn, New York, must be considered armed and extremely dangerous. Request Central make photo distribution and city-wide BOLO."

"10-4, First Squad."

"What now, Lou?"

"Now, we need to find his wife . . . fast. It's not only possible she's an accomplice, though I doubt it, but she may know where her husband is. I'm also concerned she might be in danger . . . if he hasn't killed her already."

"That makes sense, Lou, especially if the husband, for whatever reason, is intent on killing everyone in this group we've uncovered—perhaps a cult—who may have been meeting to drink each other's blood."

Martelli nodded. He reached into his pocket and pulled out his cell phone. A quick swipe of the screen brought up his address book, and with a few more taps, he was talking with Dugan again.

"Lou, we have to stop meeting this way. My girlfriend is going to be very jealous, and if she puts off our wedding next month, you're going to be in a world of hurt!"

"Hell, I wouldn't mess with either of you, Missy. Steph and I have already bought your wedding present, and we can't return it." He laughed.

Martelli turned to O'Keeffe and covered the cell phone. "What's that, Sean?"

O'Keeffe whispered something in his ear.

"Missy, Sean wants to know if he can bring Dr. Allerton to the wedding. He knows he accepted only for himself, but, ah, there've been some changes in his life."

"Tell him the answer is 'yes,' but I'm going to reveal all his secrets to her at the reception."

"He says 'good luck' to you."

"Oh, yeah? Tell him he's a dead man."

"Okay, look, darlin', I'd love to banter with you all day, but right now, we need information!"

"I'm ready. Waddaya need?"

"Look in the DMV database, first for Mariam Harandi, and then, for Jafar Harandi. What do you see?"

"They're both listed at the same address in Brooklyn."

"Shoot the data to my phone. It may or may not be correct. Sometimes people move and don't update their records with the DMV."

"Roger, that."

"Just in case, do a search covering the five boroughs for all persons with the name 'Mariam Harandi.' I need to find her as quickly as possible. My gut tells me she's in danger."

"Done."

"Already? How many 'Mariam Harandis' did you find?"

"Seventeen."

"Damn. How many live in Brooklyn."

"Five."

"Okay, Missy, send the data for all 17 people to my cell phone."

"On the way."

"Good. Now, check the five boroughs for Jafar Harandi."

"Seven."

"And in Brooklyn?"

"Just the one we found in the DMV records. Lou."

Martelli did not say anything. His mind was racing.

"Lou, you still there?"

"This isn't good, Missy. Chances are he's not at that address, which is going to make finding him difficult.

"Send me what you have. We'll start at the last address we have for Mariam Harandi and work our way through all of the data on people by that name, if we have to, until we find her."

"Will do."

"Talk with you later."

"Bye, Lou."

"Lou, what do you want to do about Faraz Tehrani?"

Even before O'Keeffe had finished speaking, Martelli was speed dialing Deputy Coroner Antonetti.

"Michael. Martelli."

"Not another one, Louis."

"Oh, yes . . . Faraz Tehrani, died just before Christmas, 2009. His wife said he passed from a heart attack, but—"

"You suspect he was poisoned."

"Absolutely. Get a court order and exhume the body, if you would. And do what you can to ensure that everyone is as sensitive as possible when talking to Mrs. Tehrani."

"I assure you, Michael . . . it will be handled with the utmost sensitivity."

■ *Theodore Jerome Cohen*

Thirty

"Michael, it's Lou. I need to talk with you for a few minutes." While O'Keeffe drove to the last known address for Mariam Harandi, Martelli took the opportunity to seek information on the disease that killed the woman's daughter.

"What can you tell me about thalassemia major?"

"It's a horrible disease, Louis . . . absolutely horrible. Babies born with it are well at birth because they possess a special form of hemoglobin found in fetuses and newborns. But before long, usually by the end of the first year, the child's red blood cells, which have a genetic defect, are unable to produce normal hemoglobin. Are you with me so far?"

"Yes. Please go on."

"Okay. Now, red blood cells use hemoglobin to carry oxygen to tissues. So, because of the defective hemoglobin in the child's body, most forms of thalassemia produce chronic, lifelong anemia."

"How does it affect the child?"

"Well, if it's not treated, of course, the child dies. And there is no cure . . . doctors can only relieve the symptoms."

"How is that done?"

"With blood transfusions, which create other problems."

"Like you said, Michael, it's a horrible disease."

"Oh, yes. Even when the disease is under control, children suffering from thalassemia major usually are pale and irritable. They may also be jaundiced and have their growth retarded."

"Thanks, Michael. I guess Steph and I should count our blessings for the two healthy children we have."

"Do it every day, Louis."

"By the way, I know it's still early in the day, but can you tell me anything about the Duval woman?"

"I've just about completed the autopsy. However, I don't have the tox screens back yet. I can tell you this, though . . . she died of a massive coronary. And the stake found in her heart did *not* kill her. It was embedded postmortem. Interestingly, it was fashioned from ash, which is the preferred wood in Russia and the Baltic for destroying vampires."

"So, do you think we may have another case, here, in which the victim was poisoned by someone who first injected her with snake venom?"

"I was just getting to that. There's a small mark just beneath, and to the rear of, her right earlobe. I'd say it's the entry site for the hypodermic used to administer whatever was used to kill her.

"I took a skin sample from that area and sent it to the lab. We should have the results shortly. I asked them to focus on the venom of the Philippine Cobra. If I'm correct, testing should go very quickly. If we don't get a hit on that venom, then we'll have to run the full battery of tests."

"I understand. Anything else?"

"Yes, the bruise on her arm was premortem. Someone drew blood from her body before she died. They were pretty sloppy about it, too. There's no knowing what they did with it."

"I don't even want to venture a guess.

"Thanks, Michael. Please let me know the minute you hear something on the test."

■ *Theodore Jerome Cohen*

Thirty-one

'This should be the house, Lou." O'Keeffe pulled to the curb in front of a decaying two-story home in an older section of Brooklyn. With the exception of an elderly man who was walking a dog, the street was deserted. Many of the homes appeared vacant and for sale, and parking places on the street were plentiful.

The men got out of the car and walked up the stairs to the porch of the duplex. They could hear the chimes sound when O'Keeffe pushed the button to the right of the front door. Within a minute the curtain covering the window in the door parted, revealing the face of a swarthy, middle-aged man with a thick black mustache. The men displayed their badges, whereupon the man unlocked the door, opened it a few inches, and peered at them.

"Yes? What do you want?"

"My name is Detective Louis Martelli. My partner is Detective O'Keeffe. We're looking for Jafar and Mariam Harandi. Do they live here?"

"There's no one here by that name." The man spoke with a heavy Middle Eastern accent.

"What is your name, sir?"

"My name is not important."

"Look, we're not here for any other reason but to ask questions regarding the Harandis. We're not from

167

Immigration, we're not looking for drugs . . . we're just looking for the Harandis.

"Now, we can talk here, on your porch, or we can all go downtown and talk there. So I'm going to ask you again, nicely, what is your name?"

"Abrahem Jobrani."

"Mr. Jobrani, have you seen, or have you at least heard of, the Harandis?"

"I believe they lived here at one time."

"And how do you know this?"

"When we moved into this house, we had problems with rats. I asked the neighbors why we were having so many problems—one of my grandchildren was even bitten—and they said it was because the Harandis kept snakes in the basement."

"Did the neighbors ever mention why the Harandis moved out or where they might have gone?"

"No, the only thing they said was they thought the landlord might have wanted them out because of the problem the rats were causing, but no one knew for sure. You can talk with Mrs. Siavashi across the street—"

Jobrani pointed to the home immediately opposite his.

The detectives turned around. "Do you mean the brick house with the trees on either side of the walkway?" asked O'Keeffe.

"Yes, that's the one. She's quite elderly, so I'm sure she's home. Talk with her. She knows everything that goes on in this neighborhood."

The men thanked him, turned, walked across the street and up the walkway to the porch of Mrs. Siavashi's house, where Martelli rang the doorbell.

This time it took several minutes before they received a response. As the curtain covering the glass window in the front door slowly parted, they saw a frail, elderly woman who could not been more than 4-feet 6-inches in height. She was wearing a burqa, though they could see her entire face. The men displayed their badges, and she opened the door and beckoned them to come inside.

"Please, come in and have a seat."

Martelli and O'Keeffe followed her into the front room, where they sat on the couch in front of the large bay window overlooking the porch.

"May I bring you some coffee? I just brewed a fresh pot."

"That would be fine."

She shuffled into the kitchen, returning minutes later with a porcelain pot, two cups and saucers, and a tray of homemade koloocheh.

Martelli took one bite of a cookie and exclaimed, "This is the most delicious walnut cookie I have ever tasted!"

The woman's eyes lit up. It must have been music to her ears.

Martelli washed the last of the cookie down with her strong black coffee, wiped his mouth with the linen napkin she had provided, and gently began asking questions.

"First, thank you so much for your hospitality. Now I'll have to spend extra time in the gym tomorrow to get rid of the calories."

They laughed.

Martelli continued. "The reason we are here, Mrs. Siavashi, is that we need to find the Harandis to ask them some questions."

"Oh, them," she said, waving her right hand. "Troublemakers.

"I always believed they were cursed." She lowered her voice to a whisper. "Evil things went on over there."

"What makes you say that?"

"Well, first, there were the snakes."

"How do you know about them? Did you ever see them?"

"No, but the boys in the neighborhood did. They were attracted to the basement windows at night by the blue lights used to keep the snakes warm."

"Did the boys ever mention how many snakes were being kept in the basement or describe the snakes to you?"

"No, they just said that there were many, and they were different from one another . . . some were small, and some were large. One night, they said, they saw Mr. Harandi feed a rabbit to a huge snake that was kept in what appeared to be a very large plastic enclosure."

"Sounds like it might have been a Boa constrictor, Lou," commented O'Keeffe.

Martelli nodded. "Did the boys mention anything else, Mrs. Siavashi?"

"Oh, yes. They said they also saw Mr. Harandi holding a snake's head over a glass jar, with the fangs protruding into the jar. What do you suppose he was doing, Detective?"

"Sean, would you please answer Mrs. Siavashi's question."

"What Mr. Harandi was doing, ma'am, was extracting the snake's venom. This is done for a variety of reasons, including the production of anti-venom. So, it's difficult to know what Mr. Harandi was going to do with that particular specimen."

"Well, whatever it was," Mrs. Siavashi asserted, "I'm sure it was not good."

O'Keeffe shot Martelli a knowing glance.

Martelli tilted his head. "Why do you say that?"

"Because he had an evil eye. He never once talked to anyone in the neighborhood, never once performed a kind act. He was not a good man. I never saw him smile."

"Can you tell us anything about his wife?"

"She is a beautiful woman. I often saw her during the day, taking care of their little girl, poor thing. But the wife always left the house around 6 PM and never returned before 1 AM the next morning.

"And the music. Always the music, all day long. You would know it as music for the belly dance. I know it as music for raqs sharqi. Drums, finger cymbals, tambourines. Over and over again. She probably was even dancing to it . . . perhaps with snakes draped around her body."

Martelli's cell phone rang. He rose and excused himself while O'Keeffe and Mrs. Siavashi continued to chat about the art of belly dancing.

"Yes, Michael."

"Louis, the toxicology results just came back from the lab. Duval was definitely killed by a lethal dose of Philippine Cobra venom."

"I'm not surprised. And from what we just learned, it's all pointing to Jafar Harandi as the murderer. I'm not sure what his motive was, but he certainly had means and opportunity. We just learned that he kept snakes in the basement of the home he and his wife previously rented in Brooklyn. Where he keeps the snakes now, and where the Harandis currently live, are things O'Keeffe and I need to find out, and fast . . . before he strikes again."

■ *Theodore Jerome Cohen*

Thirty-two

'**I'm** sorry, I had to take that call," said Martelli, as he returned to the conversation. "Let's see, where were we? Ah, yes, we were talking about Mrs. Harandi.

"You said you would see her leave her home at 6 PM and return the following morning around 1 AM. What do you think she was doing during the time she was gone?"

"I guess she was working, Detective."

"Doing what?"

"I don't know. Perhaps belly dancing? Every once in a while I would look out my window and see her taking hangers holding what looked to be colorful costumes into the house. She must have had them dry cleaned."

"Did you ever talk to her, perhaps on the street, and ask her about her work?"

"I would see her on the street from time to time. We would talk about the weather and what was happening in the neighborhood. We usually met when she was taking her daughter for a walk. That dear child . . . it was just a tragedy what happened to her. But no, she never mentioned what she did for a living or where she worked. And there didn't seem to be a nice way of bringing the subjects up."

O'Keeffe picked up the conversation at this point.

"So, what can you tell us about the daughter?"

"Salomea was her name. She was a beautiful child, but very sickly. She always looked pale. And she was short for her age, too."

"That's what we heard."

"You know, she died in 2009, shortly after New Year's Day, a few months after the Harandis moved out."

"Moved out? Why?"

"Well, I heard a rumor they had broken up. But some people thought the landlord had asked them to leave because of the snakes and the rats the snakes attracted. It didn't matter. Everyone was happy to see them leave."

"So, if what you heard was true, you would think Mrs. Harandi took the child with her?"

"Oh, yes. She doted over that child. But no one knows where she went."

"And Mr. Harandi?"

"No one knows what happened to him either."

Sean pressed on. "Did Mrs. Harandi ever mention what her husband did for a living?"

"Once, when he was late for work and left the house in a hurry while Mrs. Harandi and I were standing outside talking, she said he was an expert on Middle Eastern antiquities and was often asked by libraries and museums to help them purchase old books, maps, and paintings. She also told me he was a recognized expert on periods going back centuries before the birth of Christ."

Martelli nodded. "One last question, Mrs. Siavashi. Did the Harandis entertain much?"

"Not often. But every four or five months, or so, they appeared to have a party. It always upset everybody on the block because strangers would park in places the residents wanted to use for their own cars."

"Were these parties held on the weekends?"

174

"No, not always. Sometimes they were held during the week."

"Do you have any idea how many people attended?"

"I don't know. I watched out my window on one or two occasions . . . maybe eight or ten people at the most would come to the house. Sometimes two or more would come in the same car. I saw both men and women."

"Thank you, Mrs. Siavashi. This has been most helpful."

The men stood. Martelli shook Mrs. Siavashi's hand, as did O'Keeffe.

"Would you like to take some koloocheh with you?"

She didn't have to ask twice.

■ *Theodore Jerome Cohen*

Thirty-three

'Well, Sean, we have a choice. Either we can go back to the First and start dialing for dollars, trying to find Mariam Harandi, the belly dancing wife of the suspect Jafar, or we can start ringing doorbells at the houses of every 'Mariam Harandi' in the New York area. Beyond the BOLO that we've already put out on her husband, I don't know if we have any other options. What's your call?"

"Let's get Dugan started on generating a list of nightclubs within a 50-mile radius of New York City featuring belly dancing and see if we can't find this 'Mariam' lady."

"Agreed."

Martelli reached into his suit coat, withdrew his cell phone, and speed dialed Dugan.

"Lou! Wazup, man?"

Martelli laughed. "You sound like my kids."

"You gotta keep up with the lingo, dude. It's the only way to stay young."

"Listen, darlin', can you pull together a list of every nightclub or other type of establishment within 50 miles of the city that features belly dancing?"

"Why? Are you planning a bachelor party for Sean?" He heard her laugh.

"Nooo . . . we need to find Mariam Harandi. As best we can tell, she makes her living as a belly dancer. The question is, where does she work? It might be easier and faster to locate her by calling around and finding her place of employment rather than by visiting every 'Mariam Harandi' in the greater-New York City area. Sean and I are heading back to the First now to do that."

"Brilliant idea. This must be the reason they pay you the big bucks!!!"

"Actually, it was Sean's idea."

"He's the man! I'll have the list in your e-mail before you return to the precinct."

"Thanks."

"Oh yeah, one last thing . . . Alexa and I have been through Duval's documents."

"Find anything interesting?"

"We found e-mails tying her to Hayes, but you already knew about that connection. One e-mail mentioned Mariam and Jafar Harandi splitting up . . . it was dated September 17, 2008. It also mentioned the fact that their group would not be meeting again until Mariam found a new place to live."

"Obviously she found a place quickly, Missy, because they were back in business by early November."

Martelli thought for a moment. "I wonder why they split up."

"I don't know, Lou. But I'm sure you're going to ask when you find her."

Thirty-four

Martelli and O'Keeffe returned to the First Precinct shortly before noon, and after grabbing a quick sandwich at a local deli, headed for Martelli's office to print out the list of establishments Dugan had provided where belly dancing was featured.

"Here you go," said Martelli, handing his partner half the stack.

"There must be a hundred listings here, Lou."

"That's my guess. But I think with the two of us hitting the phones, we might get lucky. This should be a close-knit community. I would expect most dancers are ethnic Middle Easterners, and they probably know of one another, if not know each other directly. You know what to ask. Just use your personal cell phone so you don't scare anyone off if they were to see NYPD on their caller ID."

O'Keeffe went back to his office, which was next to Martelli's, and the men set about their work.

At first, the going was slow. It was the lunch hour, and reaching the managers with whom they needed to speak was difficult. As well, some establishments had yet to open, given that they catered to a crowd that did not arrive for dinner and entertainment until well after 8 PM. But they pressed on, chatting up the people with whom they spoke, pretending to be old boyfriends of Mariam Harandi, whom they said they knew before she was married.

Hours went by without a lead. And then, shortly after 6 PM, O'Keeffe struck gold!

"Hi, can I speak with the manager, please?"

"I'm the manager. May I help you?"

"Yes, my name is Sean O'Keeffe. I'm in town from Miami for a few days, and I was hoping to find an old girlfriend of mine. We dated years ago, before she was married. Her name is Mariam. I think she married a man by the name of Jafar Harandi, but it's been a few years, so I may have the name wrong. Anyway, she used to work as a belly dancer, and I thought someone in your restaurant might know her."

"Oh, yes, Mariam Harandi. I think one of our dancers, Saltanah Amiri, used to work with her. But she's not in right now. She doesn't start work until 8 PM. You could call here then, and perhaps she would have a minute to talk with you before her first set."

"That would be wonderful. Thank you so much. It would great to see Mariam again. I'll be sure to get back to Miss Amiri. By the way, what is your name?"

"I'm Edesa Amiri."

"Oh, are you sisters?"

She laughed. "No, our families lived in the same town when the Shah of Iran decreed that we must have last names."

O'Keeffe laughed. "I bet you've been asked that question a million times."

"Mr. O'Keeffe, you can't imagine how confusing it is to most people."

They laughed. "Well, thank you again, Miss Amiri. I'll be sure to contact Saltanah later today for the information I need."

O'Keeffe almost tripped over his trash bin as he raced around his desk, out the door, and into Martelli's office.

Martelli was on the phone, schmoozing up someone in an attempt to elicit information on Mariam Harandi. It looked as if he was coming up empty handed.

O'Keeffe started waving his hands wildly over his head. Martelli knew instantly what he was going to say. Terminating his call, Martelli threw his hands in the air, palms up. "Lay it on me."

"I found someone who knows Harandi."

"Who is it?"

"A belly dancer named Saltanah Amiri. She works at the Zamani's Persian Restaurant and Lounge on the Upper East Side. But she doesn't get in until shortly before 8 PM.

"What do suggest we do, Sean?"

"Look, it's getting into the dinner hour. We're going to start having problems reaching the people we need to talk to, assuming they'll even take time to talk to us if we can get them to the phone. Why don't we grab a bite, drive to Zamani's, bide our time, and confront Miss Amiri when she shows up for work. If she knows where Mariam Harandi is, we'll shoot right over to see her. In the best of all worlds, this could be the end of the chase . . . at least as far as Mariam Harandi is concerned."

181

■ *Theodore Jerome Cohen*

Thirty-five

Martelli pulled his unmarked car into the No Parking zone in front of Zamani's Persian Restaurant and Lounge, much to the consternation of the valet parking attendant. O'Keeffe jumped out, flashed his badge, and sprinted into the restaurant's foyer. Martelli stayed in the car.

The restaurant's hostess, a young woman whose name badge read 'Parisa,' was dressed to evoke images of a harem girl straight out of a Persian fairy tale. She smiled as O'Keeffe approached.

"Hi. I'm Sean O'Keeffe. I spoke with Edesa earlier today. She said that Saltanah Amiri might be able to tell me where I could find an old girlfriend. Do you think Saltanah might have just a minute to talk with me?"

"Sure. Give me a minute. I'll see if she can step out here."

The woman disappeared through thick velvet curtains that had been strung across a door at the back of the restaurant. It did not take her two minutes to reappear together with a beautiful dark-haired woman dressed as a belly dancer.

"This is Saltanah Amiri, Mr. O'Keeffe."

"Thank you."

"Good evening, Miss Amiri. My name is Sean O'Keeffe. Can we sit over there for a few minutes?" He motioned to some chairs located on one side of the foyer."

"Of course, Mr. O'Keeffe. Parisa tells me you are looking for an old girlfriend."

They sat.

"Actually, Miss Amiri, I'm a police officer." He showed her his badge.

"Oh my! Am I in some kind of trouble?"

He laughed, gently. "No. I just want to talk with you for a minute."

She put her right hand to her chest and breathed a sigh of relief.

"I need to speak with Mariam Harandi, and I'm told you might know where she can be found."

"I'm sorry, Detective, I don't know where she lives, if that's what you're asking. But the last time I spoke with her, she was working as a belly dancer and snake charmer under the name 'Lilith' at a lounge on Long Island . . . I think it's called Aliaabaadi's Arabian Nights Restaurant."

"Thank you so much, Miss Amiri. I see Parisa's trying to get your attention. I guess it's time for you to perform. Have a good evening."

Saltanah Amiri ran to the stage to begin her performance as O'Keeffe pushed open the restaurant's front door and jogged to the waiting *Crown Vic*. As he approached, he gave Martelli a 'thumbs up.' His partner smiled broadly.

"Where to, Sean?"

"Aliaabaadi's Arabian Nights Restaurant, on Long Island. Do you know where it is?"

"No, but I'm sure you can get some directions to it on your telephone."

"You bet."

It took O'Keeffe only a few seconds to bring up a map on his cell phone. Martelli took one look, checked for traffic behind him before pulling out, and then headed for Long Island and the town of Woodmere. The restaurant was located off Rockaway Boulevard. In 25 minutes, they pulled into the parking lot. It was a short walk to the entrance.

The evening's first performance was in full swing.

"Holy shit, look at the size of that snake."

On the stage, a huge Boa constrictor had wrapped itself around the torso and shoulders of a beautiful brunette of Middle Eastern heritage. Dressed in a traditional belly dancing costume, she had almond-colored eyes and long brown hair that fell to her waist. The two-piece costume, purple and gold in color, was covered in sequins and simulated jewels.

Two bare-chested male handlers, dressed in loose-fitting red harem pants and gold slippers with white turbans atop to their heads, stood to either side of her. They were there as much to assist in handling the snake as to provide help in the event the reptile became nervous or insecure and began to squeeze. Whether the daggers housed in the gold sheathes lodged within their waistbands were there for use in an emergency or for effect is something O'Keeffe did not appear eager to know.

Martelli shook his head. "How'd you like to make your living doing that?"

"I'd have to change my shorts at least five times a night!"

"What is it that makes you nervous, Sean? The woman?"

"Very funny!"

The men watched as the dancer manipulated the snake, a 6-foot, 12-pound Rainbow Boa, around her arms and hands. As she bent backwards, the snake moved toward her face. The dancer then rose, wrapping the snake around her waist

185

before gently guiding the reptile to encircle her legs as it moved to the floor.

"Will there be just the two of you, gentlemen?"

It was the hostess. She caught the men by surprise.

"Oh, we were just passing through on a business trip," said Martelli. "My friend hasn't seen Mariam for many years—he used to date her, you know—so we thought we'd catch her show and say 'hello.'"

She looked at Sean. "How nice of you. Well, that's her performing now, as you know. Isn't she sensational? She always plays to a full house, and tonight is no exception. We're so fortunate to have her. If you'd like to have a drink at the bar, I'm sure she would be happy to meet with you in her dressing room when she's finished."

O'Keeffe nodded and thanked the women profusely. He and Martelli then made their way to the bar. Being on duty, a Pepsi was about the only drink they could order. But it gave them the cover they needed while they sat and waited for Miriam Harandi, aka 'Lilith,' to complete her act.

Harandi finished dancing to a cacophony of drums, finger cymbals, and tambourines. The applause was thunderous. As she took bow after bow, her attendants moved the snake into the large woven basket that was used to transport the reptile between her dressing room and the stage.

The snake handlers had just left Harandi's dressing room when Martelli and O'Keeffe knocked on the door.

"Come in."

The men entered. O'Keeffe looked toward the right side of the room. The snake lay on the floor of its enclosure, which was heated with a shielded heat lamp. Entrance to the enclosure was through a large door that slid up and down on two steel rails. *Thank God it's locked at the top,* he thought. *I can't stand snakes.*

186

"Mrs. Harandi?"

"Yes? Do I know you?"

"No, ma'am, we haven't met. I'm Detective Louis Martelli of the New York Police Department. My partner is Detective Sean O'Keeffe." The men displayed their badges. "May we speak with you, please? It's about matters of the utmost importance?"

"Why, certainly, Detectives. I have an hour before my next performance, so there's plenty of time to talk. Please. Have a seat." She motioned toward two chairs at the side of the room.

The men moved the chairs closer to her dressing table and sat. They both took out pens and notebooks.

Martelli began the conversation. "Mrs. Harandi, I'd like to begin by asking if you know a man by the name of Byron Hayes."

"Oh, my God, yes. Poor Byron. He was a dear friend of many years. He was murdered a year ago in Riverside Park. Why do you ask?"

"I'll explain in a moment. Let me ask you this, first.

"Do you know a man named Faraz Tehrani?"

"Why yes. He used to cash checks for my daughter. The checks were birthday gifts given to her by a friend of ours. Faraz died of a heart attack just before Christmas about two years ago."

"Yes, we know. But we now have reason to believe Mr. Tehrani also was murdered—"

Harandi, gasping for air, clutched her hands to her chest.

Martelli continued. "And he was killed in such a way as to make it look as if he suffered a heart attack.

"Do you know a man by the name of Phillip Weston and or a woman by the name of Felicia Duval?"

The blood drained from Harandi's face. "My God, has something happened to them?"

"They've also been murdered . . . and recently."

Harandi looked panic-stricken. She shut her eyes and trembled. Then she started to sob.

Martelli reached to her dressing table, grabbed several tissues, and forced them into her hands.

No one said anything for a minute.

Finally, Martelli broke the silence. "What aren't you telling us, Mrs. Harandi?"

She shook her head. "I don't want to talk about it. I *can't* talk about it!"

Martelli waited a few seconds. Then, gently, he said, "Mrs. Harandi, we know about your vampire cult . . . we know you were drinking each other's blood."

She looked up, her masquera and heavy makeup running down her cheeks.

"How do you know about it?"

"From the evidence we found on some of the victim's computers."

She nodded.

"How long have you been doing it?"

"About 15 years, Detective. My husband and I started drinking each other's blood shortly after we got out of college. He had majored in Middle Eastern cultures at the American Middle Eastern University in Amman, Jordan, where I also studied. It was there he took a great interest in Ancient Mesopotamia—Sumer, Babylon, Assyria. The story of Lilith, a character from Jewish mythology, absolutely fascinated him."

Martelli's ears perked up. "I know a little about Lilith. She was considered a demon that often was depicted as living on the blood of babies."

"It's interesting you should say that, Detective. Jewish folklore portrays Lilith as Adam's first wife. She was said to have been created from the same earth as Adam, as opposed to Eve, who was created from Adam's rib. And yes, the Jews regarded her as evil. But that said, Jewish folklore has it that Lilith was forced by three angels to swear she would not harm mothers and children."

"But you never hear of Lilith in the Garden of Eden."

"No, she left Eden because she refused to become subservient to Adam. Anyway, it's the Assyrian lilitû that were said to prey upon children and women.

"As you can imagine, Detective, there are many, *many* different stories and interpretations associated with the mythological character Lilith."

"So, why did you take the name 'Lilith' when you began dancing for a living?"

"I didn't. My husband suggested it. First, he was enamored of the name, given his academic studies and interest in the many legends that had grown up around the character. Second, he simply thought it was appropriate, given our interest in vampirism. Besides, it's a beautiful name, is it not, Detective? It means 'of the night,' which was appropriate, given my work."

Martelli nodded. "So, how did it all begin . . . this drinking of blood?"

"Jafar and I started experimenting by drinking each other's blood. Then, we invited a few very close friends we knew from our university days to join us. But they didn't find it something they wanted to do, and for several years, it simply was something my husband and I did."

"But then something must have changed, did it not?"

"Oh, yes. Through his work with the New York Public Library, Jafar began to work with people who he learned had

189

similar interests in vampirism. As well, he learned of library patrons who shared his intense interest in the literature of vampires and who eagerly sought out works from the archival literature.

"Through his discussions with these people, he discovered some were as interested in tasting human blood as we were. So, we formed a small group and began meeting at our home a few times during the year to practice the art. We even found others, quite by accident, mind you, who were interested. The man who cashed checks for a living, Faraz Tehrani, came to some of our meetings."

At this point, O'Keeffe took over the questioning. "So, Mrs. Harandi, all together, how many people were in the group besides you and your husband, Hayes, Weston, Duval, and Tehrani?"

"Over the last several years, the group was stable. There were nine of us."

"Who were the other three, and where do they live?"

"Well, I can give you their names, but we haven't met since Byron was killed, so I can't vouch for where they might be today."

"That's okay . . . we'll locate them. Please go on."

"Well, the first is Paul Madison. I think he lived in Brooklyn, close to where we used to live. The other two, and I'm pretty sure they lived in Manhattan, are Carole Winters and David Feldman.

"We didn't do anything illegal, Detectives. We are . . . were . . . consenting adults. We didn't harm anyone."

"It's not our job to judge you, Mrs. Harandi," said Martelli. "We're just attempting to solve these murders."

She seemed relieved to hear these reassuring words.

Martelli continued. "Let me ask you this, however, Mrs. Harandi—"

"Yes?"

"You seemed extremely upset when I asked you about Weston and Duval? Why was that?"

A look of panic again crossed her face. She appeared as if she were hiding something so heinous that the mere mention of it would forever cast her and her family as well as anyone associated with them into the depths of Hell.

"Mrs. Harandi, believe me when I tell you we are here to gather what information we can pertaining to the Hayes, Weston, Duval, and Tehrani murders. What we discuss here will be held in the strictest of confidence. I assure you, no one outside the Police Department will have access to this information. Even within the Department, access will be severely limited."

"Knowing what you've learned, Detectives, I'm sure you know by now that my husband and I had a daughter born with thalassemia major. She was a beautiful child, my Salomea. But she became seriously ill within a year of her birth because my husband and I are carriers of a defective gene that caused a mutation in her blood."

The men nodded.

"As she grew up, Salomea needed frequent transfusions to keep her alive. Seeing this, my husband became increasingly despondent. Soon, he obsessed over her.

"As she became sicker and the need for transfusions increased, he accused our group of drinking the child's blood. Can you imagine? He said the reason she needed more and more transfusions was because we were drinking Salomea's blood while he was at work.

"It never happened, Detectives. *Never!* Believe me when I say, we *never* would have done that. Not to my dear Salomea."

191

Martelli put his hand on her arm to calm her. "I believe you, Mrs. Harandi."

"My husband became totally delusional, Detective. I tried to reason with him. I even asked Salomea's doctor to talk with him. But Jafar wouldn't listen. He was totally irrational. He even threatened to kill all of us if we didn't stop what he imagined we were doing. It got to the point where I no longer knew the man I had married. He had turned into a monster. I feared for my life."

"Go on, please," said Martelli.

"One day, while he was working at the New York Public Library, I packed my suitcases and fled, taking my daughter with me. I never saw him again.

"Not long after that, a friend told me he had been evicted from the house because his snakes attracted rats to the basement."

"So, what frightened you a few minutes ago, Mrs. Harandi, was the thought that if this story got out, people would think you and the people in your group had been drinking your daughter's blood. Further, they would conclude this was the reason your child died."

"Yes," she said in a whisper. "And there's more."

"More?"

"My husband not only threatened to kill all of the people in our group, but he also said he would kill the others first. Then, he said, he would come for me.

"He said that by drinking Salomea's blood, I truly had become the 'demon of the night,' and he wanted me to suffer by knowing, before he killed me, that each of the others had died, one by one, for the crimes they committed against his daughter."

She began sobbing uncontrollably. O'Keeffe handed her his handkerchief.

The men waited. Finally Martelli spoke.

"Do you have any idea, *any idea at all,* where your husband is?"

She shook her head. "No. I haven't seen him since I left with my daughter. I didn't even see him at her funeral."

Martelli, exhausted, put his hands to his eyes and rubbed them.

"Mrs. Harandi, is there anyplace you can stay tonight until we can check on the whereabouts of the other three individuals you mentioned? I'm concerned about your safety."

"I can stay at my boyfriend's place in the Bronx."

"Please call him now. I think it would be best if he picked you up as soon as possible. I'll speak with your boss, if you'd like?"

"That won't be necessary, Detective. I'll just tell him I'm not feeling well. One of the other girls can fill in for me. I've filled in many times for them when they wanted to go out on dates."

"All right. We'll stay here until he arrives and see you both off. And here's my card. Detective O'Keeffe will give you his, as well. If you're in the least bit concerned about anything . . . *anything at all* . . . I want you to call us immediately."

■ *Theodore Jerome Cohen*

Thirty-six

It was approaching 10 PM when Martelli and O'Keeffe finally got on the road and headed back to the First Precinct. "Sorry, Steph, I have to take Sean back to the city to pick up his car. And I need to check out some things at the office before I come home. Don't wait up for me, okay?"

"All right, Honey. I'll leave a sedative on your bed stand with a glass of water. It'll help you sleep. What time do you want me to set the alarm for? The usual?"

"Yeah, that'll be fine. How are the kids?"

"They're great. Tiffany's team won the debate, and Rob aced the science test. Despite our best efforts, Lou, I think they're going to turn out okay after all."

They laughed. Being a cop was difficult. Being a cop's wife was, at times, even more demanding.

"I'll see ya later. Love you."

"Love you, too."

"You have a wonderful marriage, Lou. I really mean it."

"Thanks, Sean. Perhaps someday you'll find the woman who's right for you."

They drove in silence.

All of a sudden, Sean turned to Lou. "What the hell did you mean, 'I need to check out some things at the office?'"

Martelli laughed. "I wondered how long it would take for you to come alive on that."

"You're going to check on Madison, Winters, and Feldman, aren't you?"

"Why Sean O'Keeffe, did anyone ever tell you what a great detective you would make? Wanna take a look with me?"

"Of course. Do you think I'm gonna let you take all the credit for cracking these case on your own?"

Thirty-seven

Martelli parked in front of the First Precinct, and the men walked toward their offices. "Want some coffee, Lou?"

"Only if it's freshly brewed. At this hour, you probably could stand a spoon up in the brew pots, assuming there's even coffee in them."

"I know. More often than not, the bottoms of the damn things contain nothing but caramelized gunk it'll take someone an hour to clean out."

Martelli went to his office. After a quick pass through his e-mail, he signed on to the *New York Times,* brought up the obituaries, and began searching for the three people whose names Harandi have given them.

"Here's your coffee . . . freshly brewed, just as you like it."

"Thanks! I need this."

"Any luck?"

"Yes . . . unfortunately. Madison died as a result of complications following heart surgery necessitated by injuries suffered during a mugging."

"Hmmm . . . let's see." Martelli brought up the *New York Times* news archives and performed a search on Madison's name.

"Here it is . . . 'Madison was found lying on a side street near his Brooklyn home in March 12, 2010. He had been

197

attacked, mugged, and stabbed repeatedly in the heart by an assailant who made off with his watch and wallet. Police have no leads and are asking anyone . . . .' You know the rest."

"Interesting place to stab someone. What about the others."

"Stand by . . . searching for Winters now."

O'Keeffe, looking over Martelli's shoulders, took a sip of his coffee and wiped his mouth on the back of his hand.

"Oh, oh . . . here she is. 'Carole Winters, beloved daughter . . . died of cardiac arrest—'"

"When did she die, Lou?

"July 17, 2009."

Martelli turned his attention to David Feldman.

"Anything, Lou?"

"Zip."

"Which may or may not mean he's dead."

"I know. And even if he's still alive, I don't know how much more time we have until both he and Mariam Harandi are dead.

"I'll send Missy a note right now, asking her to find this guy, dead or alive." Martelli began typing furiously. "I'm also sending Antonetti an e-mail, requesting he obtain court orders to exhume the bodies of Madison and Winters. Might as well bring all the vics together in our morgue. We'll need as much evidence as we can accumulate before we close the case on Jafar Harandi?"

"Close the case on Jafar Harandi? Are you kidding? The way vics keep piling up, this is like having an annuity. You and I'll be sorting out the evidence on these cases well into the next century."

Thirty-eight

Martelli and O'Keeffe arrived at the office early the next morning to continue their review of the evidence amassed in what they now referred to as the 'Vampire Slayer Murders.' By 6 AM, Missy Dugan had already seen Martelli's e-mail from the night before and begun her computer search for David Feldman.

"Sorry, Lou. I couldn't find anything in the way of an obituary or death certificate issued in the five Boroughs during the last two years for a 'David Feldman.' Feldman sometimes is spelled with two n's, by the way, so I also checked using that spelling. Still nothing."

"So, as far as we know, he may still be alive."

"It would appear that way."

"That might buy us some time, at least as far as Mrs. Harandi is concerned. Thanks."

Martelli terminated the call and dialed Antonetti's extension.

"Louis, I was just in the process of preparing the paperwork for the exhumations for the three bodies you requested. Let's see . . . Tehrani, Madison, and Winters. How many victims does that make so far?"

"Let's see . . . and I'm assuming these all are validated on your table, Michael . . . Weston, Hayes, Duval, Tehrani, Madison, and Winders. Six to date.

"Well, maybe seven."

"Seven? Who's the seventh?"

"A guy by the name of David Feldman. We haven't been able to determine whether he's dead or alive."

"Even so, your perp isn't quite as prolific a killer as the Long Island Serial Killer. You know, he's the unidentified suspect who is believed to have murdered ten people over the last 15 years and dumped their bodies along the Ocean Parkway in Suffolk and Nassau Counties."

"Yeah, well, I don't need my perp setting any records, believe me. He's given Sean and me more than enough to do. And we know who he is, to boot. We just can't find his ass!"

"Which is something we're going to devote our time to, today . . . looking for him."

"What do you plan to do?"

"Well, it's pretty clear he still keeps snakes somewhere in the area. Which means he needs supplies . . . food, heat and UV lamps, veterinary services, things like that. That's where we're going to start."

"I wish you luck."

Martelli and O'Keeffe spent the remainder of the day canvassing reptile veterinarians, pet shops, and other establishments that catered to the sale, care, and feeding of exotic pets. While several doctors and pet shop proprietors recognized the DMV photograph of Jafar Harandi, none could provide a home address, much less a credit card receipt. Those few who remembered him recalled that he had always purchased his snakes and supplies using cash. And they never failed to add that he seemed like such a nice young man.

"What a nice guy," exclaimed O'Keeffe as he facetiously mimicked the veterinarian with whom they had just met, a young woman who had spoken glowingly of Harandi. "I wonder what the vet would have said if we told her Jafar Harandi had killed, mutilated, or desecrated six people in the last few years and now was working on his seventh."

Martelli smiled. "Tell me about it. It's always the psychopathic killer next door . . . the 'nice guy' who helps you with your groceries . . . you have to worry about."

■ *Theodore Jerome Cohen*

<u>Thirty-nine</u>

It was well past 11 PM when Martelli's cell phone rang. He and his wife had been asleep for more than an hour, the first time they had gotten to bed that early, and the first time in many days that Martelli had been able to fall asleep without the aid of a sedative. He reached to his nightstand and felt for the phone. Once found, he brought it to his face, swiped the screen with his finger, put it to his ear, and whispered "Martelli."

A frantic voice whispered, "Detective?"

"Who is this?"

"Detective, I'm frightened. This is Mariam . . . Mariam Harandi."

Martelli sat up in bed.

Stephanie turned and pulled the covers over her head. She had been through this a thousand times and knew better than to interrupt a call at that hour by asking who it was.

"What's wrong, Mrs. Harandi?"

"I'm afraid," she whispered.

"Where are you?"

"In my dressing room . . . at the club where we met the other night. Please. Come quickly. Someone's in the building."

"Is anyone with you?"

"No . . . everyone's left for the night. I stayed to change. Everything was quiet until a few minutes ago, when I suddenly heard something in the dining room. Please, please . . . come quickly."

"Lock the door to your dressing room. I'll be there as soon as I can."

Martelli terminated the call and speed dialed O'Keeffe.

"Sean, get dressed! Meet me at the club where Harandi dances. She's in trouble."

"Are you calling for backup from the local police?"

Martelli, using his shoulder to hold the phone to his head, started putting on his pants.

"No! I don't wanna do that."

"But—"

"No buts . . . I know the risks. If the locals get involved, the story will come out, the public will panic, things will blow up in the Department's face, and you and I'll be made to take the fall."

"Come on, Lou . . . Hanlon wouldn't do that to us."

"Wake up and smell the coffee, Sean! I can hear him now. 'Martelli! O'Keeffe! I didn't say you were to blame. I said I was blaming you.' Sean, you and I would be lucky if we didn't end up pounding a beat when Hanlon got through with us."

"I see your point."

"Good. Then get your ass in gear!"

"I'm on my way."

Martelli arrived at the Aliaabaadi's Arabian Nights Restaurant shortly before midnight. O'Keeffe was nowhere in sight. Two cars were parked in the parking lot, side by side. Martelli quickly picked the lock on the door to the service entrance, opened the door, and used a waste bin to prevent it from closing. *Sean will need a way into the building,* he thought.

He slipped inside, working his way through the kitchen and into the dimly lit dining room. Not a sound could be heard.

Weapon drawn, he made his way slowly up the stairs on the right side of the stage. Quietly, cautiously, he moved behind the curtain on the right wing. There, he found a stairway leading down to a hallway that led to the performers' dressing rooms.

This was familiar territory. He and O'Keeffe previously had come down this hallway to meet with Harandi after her performance, albeit having entered it further back through a door they had been shown by the hostess.

The door to Harandi's dressing room looked as if it had been forced open, and light shown through a small space between the door and its frame. Martelli put his back to the wall and inched his way down the hallway, stopping to listen between steps. There was no sound.

Once at the door, he waited a few seconds before shifting quickly to the other side, where he once again stood with his back against the wall.

What—or better, who—is behind this door? he thought. *Should I wait for O'Keeffe? What if he arrives and her husband, hearing him, kills Mariam? What if she's already dead?*

Martelli appeared to be running every possible scenario though his mind.

Inching closer to the door, he slowly lifted his left hand, and in one sharp movement, pushed the door open with the intent of startling whoever might be concealed behind it.

Instantly, someone grabbed his left arm and flung him to the floor. Before Martelli could regain his footing, the man was on top of him. He grabbed Martelli's weapon with his left hand, and almost simultaneously jabbed a hypodermic

205

needle into the detective's leg, emptying a syringe full of snake venom with the simple pump of the plunger.

That done, the attacker sprung backwards to his feet. Martelli's gun now was pointed directly *at him.*

Martelli looked to his left. Staring at him blankly through dead almond-colored eyes was Mariam Harandi, now lifeless with a dagger sticking out of her chest, just above her heart.

Turning his gaze back to his feet, Martelli saw the syringe sticking out of his leg. *You dumb shit! You stuck it into my prosthetic leg! Now the question is: how do I feign being poisoned? I need to stall so Sean has time to get here."*

"I know who you are. You're Jafar Harandi."

"I'm afraid you have the advantage over me, sir. I don't know *your* name."

"I'm Detective Louis Martelli, NYPD. I've been looking for you."

"I'll bet you have, Detective Louis Martelli, NYPD. Well, now you've found me. Aren't you going to tell me I'm not going to get away with this?"

Harandi was taunting him. Obviously he believed that *he* held the advantage. After all, he had just injected—or at least *thought* he had injected—his pursuer with a lethal dose of Philippine Cobra venom. All that remained was for Martelli to become immobile and Harandi would make good his escape.

"We're just going to wait here for a little while, my friend. It should not take long, 30 minutes at most. And then, I'll be leaving. You and my dearly departed wife, however, shall remain here. By the time they find your lifeless bodies tomorrow morning, I'll be well on my way to Bahrain.

"See?" He took several items out of his black leather jacket. "Fake passport. Fake New York drivers license. Foreign money. And Kennedy International Airport, from which my flight will leave in a few hours is just down the road.

"So, contrary to what you may think, I most certainly *am* going to get away with it."

Harandi moved closer, bent down, and reaching into Martelli's suit coat pocket, took out his cell phone, which he casually slid along the floor to the nearby wall.

Martelli looked around the room. Four feet to his left was the large plastic enclosure containing the Boa constrictor that Mariam used in her act.

Harandi saw Martelli eyeing the snake. "I see you are looking at Azarnoosh. Is she not beautiful? I raised her from a baby. Her name means 'eternal fire' in our language. Do you know she can generate 8 pounds per square inch of pressure if she were to wrap herself around you and squeeze?

"Here . . . I will let her show you how strong she is."

Harandi slowly stepped backwards, all the while holding the gun on Martelli while reaching for the chair along the wall near the door with his left hand. Finding it, he grabbed the top rail and swung the chair around to the side of the Boa's enclosure.

Harandi glanced quickly at the clipboard hung on the wall. "Ah . . . I see Azarnoosh has not been fed for a month, Detective. I'm sure she must be getting very hungry by now."

Taking the key from the hook on the wall, Harandi, using the chair as a step, climbed to the top of the enclosure and undid the lock on the door.

Martelli looked down the length of his body at the snake. *Dammit . . . where is O'Keeffe? I can't let on that I'm not poisoned or this guy will shoot me. And if I don't do something, the snake will crush me to death!*

Years of training had taught the snake that when the door was opened, she would be allowed out. Now, she heard the 'click' of the lock and saw the vertical sliding door begin to move.

The snake stirred, and slowly moved down from her platform below a shielded heat lamp to the floor, near the door.

Much to Martelli's relief, after moving only an inch, the door to the enclosure jammed. Martelli watched as Harandi started shaking it back and forth with his left hand, attempting to loosen it and raise it at least a few more inches so that the Boa could slither out.

The reptile pushed its snout out from under the door, its lips sensing the temperature of the air in the room. It would only take another few inches of clearance, and the Boa would be free.

Martelli broke out in a sweat. *Come on, Sean. Where the hell are you?* Martelli thought.

Harandi continued to shake the door, as if he were trying to 'walk it up.' But it would not budge. In complete frustration, and, perhaps, some embarrassment, he cursed in Farsi, put Martelli's gun on top of the enclosure, and placing both hands on the top of the door, began working it side to side until the snake had room to emerge from its enclosure.

Like the snake, Martelli was ready to take advantage of the situation as well. Bolting upright and reaching for his right foot, he grabbed his second service revolver from the holster on his ankle, took aim using a two-handed grip, and fired three rounds in rapid succession into Harandi's right temple. The man died instantly, his body slumping to the top of the snake's enclosure.

Martelli immediately turned to his right in an attempt to use his arms and good right leg to stand. But Boas, while known to move slowly, also can strike quickly. In an instant, the snake sprung, thrusting itself across Martelli's legs. From there, it rapidly coiled itself around the detective. The snake's sharp, twisting movements caught Martelli by surprise, and he lost his grip on the revolver, which skittered across the floor, out of reach.

Martelli struggled to uncoil the reptile from his body, but the snake was too strong. It slowly tightened its body around the Martelli, leaving him gasping for air as the snake constricted his lungs.

Suddenly Martelli heard a sharp metallic 'snap' as the bracing in his prosthetic leg gave way, throwing him off balance and onto the floor. His head hit the concrete, and the last thing he remembered seeing before blacking out was the Boa coiling its way upwards toward his head.

■ *Theodore Jerome Cohen*

Forty

'W'ake up, Lou! Dammit, wake up!" It was O'Keeffe, slapping Martelli's face, attempting to awaken him. Sirens from approaching police, fire, and rescue vehicles could be heard in the background.

Martelli stirred, groaned, and shook his head.

"What happened?"

"You must of lost your balance, fallen, and hit your head on the floor. Knocked you out cold. I got here just as the Boa was about to finish you off."

Martelli raised himself on his elbows. Around him lay pieces of the Boa constrictor. It had been hacked into large chunks by O'Keeffe using an emergency fire ax he had grabbed from a glass-windowed case on the dressing room wall. Blood poured from two bullet holes in the snake's head.

Martelli, whose head appeared to be throbbing, managed a weak smile. "I don't care what the guys at the precinct say about you, Sean, you're a pretty good shot."

"I have to be, Lou. It seems like every time we work a case lately, I have to jump in at the last minute and save your sorry ass!

"By the way, your cell phone rang while you were getting your beauty sleep." He handed the phone to his partner.

Martelli swiped the screen.

"It's a text message from Steph."

"What did she want?"
"To say goodnight and tell me she loved me."
"Are you going to tell her what happened tonight?"
"Maybe I will, and maybe I won't."
"I'll take that as a definite maybe."

<u>Epilogue</u>

Detective-Investigator Louis Martelli was placed on administrative leave with full pay pending a review of the shooting of Jafar Harandi in Lilith Harandi's dressing room at Aliaabaadi's Arabian Nights Restaurant. The shooting was subsequently judged to be 'justifiable homicide,' and Martelli was returned to duty.

It took Martelli more than two months to obtain a replacement for his damaged prosthetic leg. At first, the US Department of Veterans Affairs insisted the old one could be repaired. When Martelli protested, the government asserted that budgetary restrictions prevented them from providing a replacement. Finally, Stephanie went to their congressman, who immediately intervened on Martelli's behalf. Martelli was fitted for a new prosthesis two weeks later. That said, Martelli insists to this day it was his visit to the VA—during which he told an administrator the VA had two weeks to schedule a fitting or he would come back and stick his old leg where the sun didn't shine—that changed the government's mind.

The Weston, Hayes, Duval, and Lilith Harandi murder cases were closed, with Jafar Harandi cited as the killer of each victim.

Exhumations and examination of the bodies of Faraz Tehrani, Paul Madison, and Carole Winters found small wooden stakes had been implanted in the chest of each corpse above the place where their heart would have been. Traces of garlic were found in Tehrani's and Winters's mouths. The remains of a lemon were found in Madison's mouth. Because autopsies had been performed on Madison and Winters prior to their burial—an autopsy of Faraz Tehrani was forbidden by his Muslim faith—some skin and organ samples still were available for use in toxicology tests. The results confirmed both Madison and Winters had been poisoned with Philippine Cobra venom. Martelli and O'Keeffe concluded that the three individuals had been murdered by Jafar Harandi, and the cases were closed.

Martelli and O'Keeffe uncovered the fact that 'David Feldman' actually was Leonard David Feldmann, a Manhattan resident who used his middle name throughout his life. Feldmann, who had been murdered in 2009, originally was thought to have died while fighting off a mugger. The slug that killed him, which severed Feldmann's abdominal aorta just below the left ventricle of his heart and passed through his body, was never recovered. Exhumation of his corpse revealed traces of garlic in the oral cavity. A silver crucifix, intended as an apotropaic, had been affixed to the inside-top of Feldmann's coffin. Given the similarity between Feldmann's and Hayes's manner of death as well as the appearance of garlic in Feldmann's mouth and the crucifix in his casket, Martelli and O'Keeffe concluded that Feldmann was killed by Jafar Harandi. The case was closed.

Lake George Sheriff Geoffrey Ward is a shoo-in for re-election following his opposition's withdrawal from the race. The sheriff's surprising revelation regarding the true cause of Phillip Weston's death, with Jafar Harandi cited as the killer, not only was documented in a major case study developed by the New York State Police Crime Lab, but also, was the subject of a Letter of Commendation addressed to the sheriff and signed by the governor of New York.

Missy Dugan married her partner, Grace Palmer, in New York City following a 15-year courtship. Stephanie and Louis Martelli, Sean O'Keeffe, and Dr. Susan Allerton danced the night away, leaving the celebration well after 1 AM the following Sunday morning. Tiffany Martelli and her boyfriend, Jeffrey Romano, stayed with Dr. Allerton's daughter, Heather, for the evening at the Martelli's home in Brooklyn. Rob Martelli stayed at a friend's house for the night. O'Keeffe, waiting until the ladies had gone to the powder room together during a dance break, allowed, in good humor, that his days as a bachelor might be numbered. Martelli, in an attempt to cheer up his partner, suggested that if he were O'Keeffe, he'd see a priest as soon as possible to receive his Last Rites.

Theodore J. Cohen, PhD, holds three degrees in the physical sciences from the University of Wisconsin–Madison and has been an engineer and scientist for more than forty years. He has been an investor for more than fifty years, and most recently, has focused on investigating and reporting on corruption in US financial institutions and agencies of the US government. His seventh novel, *Lilith: Demon of the Night,* is the third in his Detective Louis Martelli, NYPD, mystery thriller series, and has to do with a serial killer who is murdering members of a modern-day vampire cult. His prior Martelli novel, *House of Cards: Dead Men Tell No Tales*, is based on real events related to the 2008 financial crisis precipitated by the housing bubble. A still earlier Martelli novel of the same genre, *Death by Wall Street: Rampage of the Bulls,* focused on corruption within the Food and Drug Administration (FDA) and the incompetence of the Securities and Exchange Commission (SEC). From December 1961 through early March 1962, Dr. Cohen participated in the 16th Chilean Expedition to the Antarctic. The US Board of Geographic Names in October, 1964, named the geographical feature Cohen Islands, located at 63° 18' S. latitude, 57° 53' W. longitude in the Cape Legoupil area, Antarctica, in his honor. Dr. Cohen's Antarctic Murders Trilogy describes what happened following a robbery of the Banco Central de Chile in Talcahuano in May, 1960. The robbery and the events that took place primarily between May 1960 and March 1962, are described in *Frozen in Time: Murder at the Bottom of the World* (Book I). *Unfinished Business: Pursuit of an Antarctic Killer* (Book II) reveals the events that unfolded between March 1962 and March 1965. *End Game: Irrational Acts, Tragic Consequences* (Book III) takes place in 1965 and resolves most, but not all, of the issues raised in the series. The Trilogy now is available as one (Kindle) edition, *Cold Blood.* Dr. Cohen's first novel, *Full Circle: A Dream Denied, A Vision Fulfilled*, which is based on his life as a violinist, was published in 2009. Dr. Cohen is a violinist in the Bryn Athyn (PA) Orchestra and particularly enjoys the music of Gustav Mahler. Dr. Cohen has published more than 350 papers, articles, columns, essays, and interviews, and is a co-author of *The NEW Shortwave Propagation Handbook* (from CQ Communications). He holds an Amateur Extra class Amateur Radio license (callsign: N4XX) and has been on the air since 1952. Finally, Dr. Cohen's analyses and opinions on Wall Street and the biotechnology industry are published under an exclusive agreement with the Internet financial site *SeekingAlpha*. For more information on Dr. Cohen and his novels, the interested reader is invited to view the book descriptions, photographs, and videos as well as listen to the interviews that can be found at <www.theodore-cohen-novels.com>.

Other Novels by
Theodore Jerome Cohen

Death by Wall Street:
Rampage of the Bulls
Praise for *Death by Wall Street*

"From the first chilling moments, *Death by Wall Street* takes the reader inside the seamy nexus of Wall Street and Washington. Theodore Cohen has written the sad and tragic tale of how US financial markets and the pharmaceutical industry have 'captured' their regulators at the SEC and the FDA. Citizens beware!! Is this fiction? Sadly, it doesn't feel like it."
Mike Krauss, author of the forthcoming novel *Pursuits of Happiness,* is a columnist and commentator with a long career in US government and politics, and international business.

"*Death by Wall Street* may be a novel, but beneath its surface lies a terrible truth: the US financial markets, together with a sleeping US government, have caused the deaths of hundreds of thousands of citizens by denying them life-saving treatments."
Kerry M. Donahue, Esq., Chief Counsel, *Care To Live*

"*Death by Wall Street* is a 'must read' for anyone who has ever wondered why investing in biotech stocks is not for the faint-hearted. What Cohen reveals about stock manipulation, the SEC, and the FDA, will shock you."
Ed Silverman, Editor and Publisher, *Pharmalot*

"Theodore Cohen, an experienced investor and respected scientist, takes us on an adventure in which he exposes the malfeasance of many on Wall Street, the ugly underbelly of hedge funds, the captured financial media, and the emasculated SEC. Strap in for a fascinating ride!"
Gregory B. Purchase, MD

"Cutting edge reporting, important insight, timely, and relevant . . . *Death by Wall Street: Rampage of the* Bulls is destined to firmly establish Theodore Jerome Cohen as a fresh voice in literary journalism. This is a book that should be added to the reading list of college and university classes in ethics, political science, finance, business, law, science, and medicine."
Richard Blake for *Readers Views*

"Similar to the writing style of Michael Crichton and Tom Clancy, Theodore Cohen adheres to short chapters laying out a mental storyboard in the reader's mind. He possesses a writing style ideal for screenplay adaptation with visuals that can make for a good movie. Why wait for Hollywood – *Death by Wall Street: Rampage of the Bulls* is currently playing in a theater near you, the theater of your mind."
Gary Sorkin for *Pacific Book Review*

For more information, visit:
www.theodore-cohen-novels.com
or your preferred on-line retailer

House of Cards:
Dead Men Tell No Tales
Praise for *House of Cards*

"Gore Vidal once observed that historians are now writing fiction and novelists are writing history. In *House of Cards: Dead Men Tell No Tales,* Theodore Jerome Cohen has written the story of the monumental greed and fraud of the banksters who have subverted the American democracy. Maybe someday, the historians will catch up to him."
Mike Krauss is a director of the Public Banking Institute and is the author of the forthcoming novel *Pursuits of Happiness*

"Cohen brings Detective Louis Martelli to a new level of shady integrity, having him become a self-appointed judge and jury of right and wrong, good and bad."
Gary Sorkin for *Pacific Book Review*

"If you enjoy the 'ripped-from-the-headline' stories of shows like *Law & Order*, then you should definitely take a ride with [Cohen's] Lou Martelli and Missy Dugan."
Marty Shaw for *Reader Views*

"A real page turner! Beware. The next terrorist attack may be on our financial systems, *if it hasn't happened already!*"
Kerry M. Donahue, Esq., Attorney at Law

For more information, visit:
www.theodore-cohen-novels.com
or www.amazon.com

Frozen in Time:
Murder at the Bottom of the World
Book I in the Antarctic Murders Trilogy
Praise for *Frozen in Time*

"A nasty little piece of skullduggery made all the more so by the fact this fictional tale is based on real events in the author's life."
Kirkus Discoveries

"Meticulously written, footnoted, including photographs, maps, memorabilia from the voyage, *Frozen in Time: Murder at the Bottom of the World* is an author's doctorate work in novel creation, hardbound with chilling cover art."
Gary Sorkin for *Pacific Book Review*

"*Frozen in Time* is compelling reading, combining the elements of conflict, suspense, intrigue, entertainment, and enlightenment. Highly recommended."
Richard R. Blake for *Reader Views*

"A fast read, with plenty of Chilean naval history and drama on the high seas in one action-packed novel full of big surprises."
Gary P. Priolo for *NavSource Naval History*

"[M]urder and mayhem blended with a dash of chilling drama!"
Deb Fowler for *Feathered Quill Book Reviews*

Frozen in Time: Murder at the Bottom of the World
Is *Recommended Reading* by Longitude®
(www.longitudebooks.com)

For more information, visit:
www.theodore-cohen-novels.com
or your preferred on-line retailer

Unfinished Business:
Pursuit of an Antarctic Killer
Book II in the Antarctic Murders Trilogy
Praise for *Unfinished Business*

"Theodore Jerome Cohen . . . is a master at creating an aura of mystery, suspense, and drama. Cohen's writing style is engaging, innovative, and focused, clearly designed for the post-modern reader."
Richard R. Blake for *Reader Views*

"It was Christmas in August as the FedEx package arrived with the 2nd of the Antarctic Murders Trilogy... [A] most enjoyable way to experience the Antarctic without having to put on a down parka."
Gary Sorkin of *Pacific Book Review*

"If you love reading a good psychological thriller and think you can stay one step ahead of a cunning murderer, you just might want to take a look at [*Unfinished Business* and] the Antarctic Murders Trilogy, a trilogy that will bring out the CSI in you!"
Deb Fowler for *Feathered Quill Book Reviews*

"Where Cohen fully succeeds is in drawing the complexity of Muñoz' character. ... With Muñoz so fully drawn, it will be a pleasure to learn his fate."
Kirkus Discoveries

Unfinished Business: Pursuit of an Antarctic Killer
Is *Recommended Reading* by Longitude®
(www.longitudebooks.com)

For more information, visit:
www.theodore-cohen-novels.com
or your preferred on-line retailer

End Game:
Irrational Acts, Tragic Consequences
Book III in the Antarctic Murders Trilogy
Praise for *End Game*

"As 'Birds of a feather flock together,' [the Antarctic Murder Trilogy] by Theodore Jerome Cohen should be packaged in a jacket and sold as a set because I certainly believe anyone hooked by the first chapter in the first novel will not be able to put this series down until all three books are finished."
Gary Sorkin for *Pacific Book Review*

"Cutting-edge drama and suspense, revealing characters through convincing dialog, provides the Antarctic Murders Trilogy with all the elements of a cutting-edge, award-winning, best-selling novel."
Richard Blake for *Reader Views*

"*End Game* will take you from the depths of an Antarctic crevasse to the top of the steeple of the Church of Saint Francis—La Iglesia de San Francisco—in search of the evil secrets of Captain Roberto Muñoz ... a man who cut his teeth at the feet of the insidious Larenas cartel!"
Deb Fowler for *Feathered Quill Book Reviews*

Jack Eadon Award for the Best Book in Contemporary Drama
Reader Views, 2011

End Game:
Irrational Acts, Tragic Consequences
Is *Recommended Reading* by Longitude®
(www.longitudebooks.com)

For more information, visit:
www.theodore-cohen-novels.com
or your preferred on-line retailer

The entire
**Antarctic Murders
Trilogy**
is available in
a <u>single</u>
Kindle edition
from
Amazon.com
as

Cold Blood

Full Circle:
A Dream Denied, A Vision Fulfilled
Praise for Full Circle

"Age is no barrier to setting goals."
Elizabeth Fisher, *Bucks County Courier Times*

"I wished wholeheartedly that it had been an autobiography! ... It is a very enjoyable read."
Elaine Richards, G4LFM, Radio Society of Great Britain (RSGB)

"*Full Circle* is an informative and accessible story that will be particularly enjoyed by musicians, electronic buffs and those who delight in family stories."
Joy Ward, *The Langhorne Ledger*

"I particularly enjoyed *Full Circle* because I identify to such a great extent with the author . . . [in music and career.]"
David Belanger, *Dials and Channels*, Journal of the Radio and Television Museum

"*Full Circle* is an inspirational read anyone, including young adults interested in amateur radio and/or music, will enjoy."
Dave Ingram, K4TWJ (SK), World of Ideas, *CQ* Magazine

For more information, visit:
www.theodore-cohen-novels.com
or your preferred on-line retailer

www.ingramcontent.com/pod-product-compliance
Lightning Source LLC
Chambersburg PA
CBHW071149170626
46809CB00002B/832